BOOK TWE

WILL BARNABAS FALL VICTIM TO DR. PEDREL'S MYSTERIOUS EXPERIMENTS?

Dr. Rudolf Pedrel, the famous scientist, is the only person in the world who can end the centuries-old curse that has made Barnabas Collins one of the living dead. At Barnabas' request, he comes to Collinwood, and sets to work perfecting the serum that will free Barnabas.

From the first, Barnabas is wary of Dr. Pedrel and suspicious of his secret projects. A series of bizarre happenings and a murder have Barnabas convinced that Dr. Pedrel is up to no good.

But Barnabas is faced with the biggest problem in his life: if he exposes the doctor, he risks not being cured, but if he doesn't, he risks being destroyed forever!

Hermes Press

Published by Hermes Press, an imprint of
Herman and Geer Communications, Inc.

Daniel Herman, Publisher
Troy Musguire, Production Manager
Eileen Sabrina Herman, Managing Editor
Alissa Fisher, Graphic Design
Kandice Hartner, Senior Editor

2100 Wilmington Road
Neshannock, Pennsylvania 16105
(724) 652-0511
www.HermesPress.com; info@hermespress.com

Book design by Eileen Sabrina Herman
First printing, 2020

LCCN applied for: 10 9 8 7 6 5 4 3 2 1 0
ISBN 978-1-61345-220-2
OCR and text editing by H + G Media and Eileen Sabrina Herman
Proof reading by Eileen Sabrina Herman and Ran Case

From Dan, Louise, Sabrina, and Jacob for D'zur and Mellow

Acknowledgments: This book would not be possible without the help and encouragement of Jim Pierson and Curtis Holdings

Printed in Canada

THE PERIL OF
BARNABAS COLLINS
by Marilyn Ross

CONTENTS

CHAPTER 1

Fog had swirled in from the ocean in the late afternoon to cloak the imposing old mansion named Collinwood in an eerie mist. In the early evening the gray mist had become so thick it was virtually impossible to see further than a dozen yards or so. The fine ocean view which the windows of the library usually offered was shut off and the wet lawns and trees ended in a shrouded world of phantoms.

The familiar grounds of the estate took on the uneasy menace of the unknown. Behind the gray fog mantle there might exist any kind of horror. And this world of ghostly mists was not a silent one. It had its own weird sounds to further heighten the mystery of it. The distant droning note of the foghorn on Collinsport Point came at regular intervals. And the strange cries of night birds circling unseen in the swirling opaque haze came like the screams of souls in torment.

It was on this eerie evening that Maggie Evans and Carolyn Stoddard worked quietly side by side in the library of Collinwood, dusting and listing the ancient volumes that lined the walls of the great room. The bookshelves filled three of the walls from floor to ceiling and the books themselves had not been given a thorough cleaning in some time. So Elizabeth, Carolyn's attractive mother, had set the two girls to the task of putting the room in order.

They had started the work earlier in the week, and because of the bad weather decided to continue their efforts on this Thursday evening. Maggie, governess to David and Amy, had always found the high-ceilinged library with its oak woodwork and musty, leatherbound volumes a fascinating place. She was intrigued with the task of going over the books.

Carolyn, who was Maggie's age, was not quite as enthusiastic. As she pulled out four heavy, dust-laden volumes and placed them on the desk she suddenly frowned.

"I sometimes think my mother deliberately selects the most unpleasant jobs for us," she sighed, pouting.

Maggie paused in dusting a shelf to glance at her with twinkling eyes. "You'd much rather be meeting your date at the Blue Whale," she said.

The other girl gave an independent shrug. "Why not?"

"For one thing, it's much too foggy to drive to the village tonight," Maggie told her. "And for another, the Blue Whale is bound to be much too crowded with all the fishermen in for the night. No boats will be going out in this fog."

Glancing towards the windows, Carolyn said, "It's miserable and spooky! I hate this late fall weather!"

"It's not all that bad. And we do have to get this work done."

"Mother could have hired someone from the village to do it," Carolyn said petulantly as she began to reluctantly dust the books she'd taken down.

"Your mother values the library and so does your Uncle Roger." Maggie reminded her. "I think it's a wonderful old room."

Carolyn smiled at her wanly. "I'll say this for you, Maggie, you do care a lot for Collinwood. Sometimes I wish it would burn down. Then we'd get a fine new house."

"You mustn't say that!" Maggie reprimanded her. She stared at the other girl with concern. "Think of all the fine things here you'd never be able to replace, like the books, the paintings and the antiques!"

"And the ghosts!" Carolyn replied. "I think there must be one for each of its forty rooms. And on a dark, gloomy night like this you sort of expect to see them all."

Maggie laughed. "You've listened too much to the villagers' superstitious stories."

"You can't very well ignore them."

"I'd make a try," Maggie advised as she reached further back to dust the wall. As she briskly rubbed the stained oak there was a sudden clicking sound and a tiny door about ten inches high by seven inches wide sprung open. Maggie gasped and drew her hand back.

"What is it?" Carolyn had heard the clicking sound and witnessed Maggie's surprised reaction.

"Some sort of secret compartment," Maggie said, giving Carolyn an awed glance. "Shall I see what's in it or call your mother first?"

"She left the job to us. I don't see why we need to bother her."

"I suppose we can speak to her about it later," Maggie said hesitantly. Then she turned and, peering into the shadows of the shelf, reached out to find what might be in the dark compartment. In a moment her hand touched what seemed to be small booklets, and she drew out a tiny stack of brown-covered notebooks neatly tied with a pink ribbon.

"Is that all there is in there?" Carolyn said, disappointed.

Maggie reached in again. "I guess so." Then she gave her attention to the bound notebooks. "These look like diaries."

"Our ancestors were always keeping them," Carolyn said. "The Collins family bred a lot of self-important individuals."

Maggie was untying the books. "I think keeping a diary is a fine idea."

"Why would anyone hide a diary in there?"

"They might not want it to be found," Maggie said, opening the first one. Her eyes scanned the neat writing in faded purple ink on the page yellowed by age. Then she told Carolyn, "This seems fascinating. It dates back to the period of Queen Victoria. It's the diary of some English girl named Diana Hastings!"

"Diana Hastings! I've never heard of her," Carolyn said.

"Nor I," Maggie agreed and she opened the other books. "They're all in the same hand. I'm going to take these up to my bedroom with me and read them before I go to sleep. I can tell your mother about them in the morning."

Carolyn gave a tiny shudder. "I wouldn't want to read any dead girl's diary on this weird kind of night. It would make me think of ghosts."

Maggie glanced at the books in her hand with a sad smile. "I'm sure Diana Hastings must have been a pleasant girl. And perhaps her spirit will be more at rest for my reading what she has written."

Carolyn picked up her duster and returned to the stack of books. "Let's not talk about it anymore. The very thought of it makes me feel creepy!"

So Maggie discreetly made no more mention of the diaries as they continued their work. But when they stopped just before ten she took the notebooks upstairs with her. She bade Carolyn goodnight in the dim light of the main hallway and entered her darkened room.

Not until she was in bed did she start to read the various notebooks. She kept her small bedside lamp on for the purpose, although its light was really inadequate. Her window was open a fraction and a slight breeze had come up, billowing the white lace curtain.

Maggie read until her eyes began to ache. When she closed the last of the diaries and snapped off the bed-lamp, she lay back on her pillow and studied the ghostly movement of the billowing white curtain in the darkness. "Like a hovering wraith," she thought as her eyes gently closed.

The thin, feminine voice came like the soft sighing of a night wind and the words were clear if faintly spoken: "Now you know something of my life in London town so long ago . . ."

It was an evening in May in the London of good Queen Victoria. The Queen was in deep mourning for the recently deceased Prince Albert, but the grief the tiny monarch felt for her dead husband was no longer shared by the populace in general. London had again become the familiar gay center of the English-speaking world. The theater was enjoying a revival and great parties and balls were the order of the day. Sadness had given away to a deliberate frivolity, and there was no more frivolous maiden in all the sprawling city than Diana Hastings. Demure and golden-haired, Diana regarded herself in the oval full-length mirror in her room with a saucy pleasure. The golden frame of the big mirror was a suitable border to set off her piquant beauty.

Her braided hair was rolled in plaits at her ears flatteringly, and her blue party dress was cut sufficiently low to show her lovely bosom. The golden locket around her throat matched the earrings dangling from dainty ears. She surveyed herself in the mirror and hoped she was truly enchanting, since tonight was to be a very special night for her.

The door to her room opened suddenly, and caught in the act of admiring herself, she turned in confusion to face the stern figure of her widowed mother. She said, "You gave me a start, Mama."

Irene Hastings had once been a beauty like Diana, but grief and grim resignation had left their mark on her face. She had never gotten over the death of her husband, a rich and elderly shipping merchant. And since the queen had made mourning fashionable, Irene Hastings had grasped it to her. She and Diana lived in a wealthy section of the city in an elegant house attended by numerous servants. But Irene Hastings seldom left the house, which made it lonely and difficult for her daughter.

The older woman in somber black eyed Diana reproachfully. "It is not fitting or modest to preen oneself before a mirror," she said.

Diana smiled ruefully. "But I do want to look well."

"You always do. But it's not necessary to make a fetish of it," her mother said. "Captain Grant is here to escort you to the ball."

"Timothy is so punctual," Diana said. "I'll be right down."

Her mother continued to stare at her. "I'm only allowing you to go since you'll have Captain Grant as an escort. And I want you to behave well and come home at an early hour."

"Yes, Mama," Diana said with a sigh.

"You know that I trust Captain Grant," her mother went on ponderously. "And I hope that you will one day be his wife."

Diana frowned. "I'm not ready to marry anyone yet!"

"You must soon make a decision," her mother warned her. "You will be very wealthy in your own right. And a woman in your position needs a husband to protect her."

"Yes, Mama," she said dutifully. "But I'd rather not discuss it tonight. I want to enjoy the party."

Her mother's eyes were cold. "Life is not meant exclusively for enjoyment," she said.

Diana followed her mother downstairs. If she had not had her own plans for the ball she would have been depressed, but she knew there would be someone there to meet her. Someone she loved! A man her mother hadn't ever heard of.

Captain Timothy Grant of the bristling black mustache and stuffy formal manners was waiting for her in the living room. Because the host of the ball in Portman Square was a military figure, all the guests of military rank were wearing dress uniform. And Timothy Grant was resplendent in his red jacket and white pants. He bowed from the waist like a wound-up toy soldier and smiled politely from behind the broad, black mustache.

"You are a delight to the eye tonight, dear Diana," he said.

"Thank you, Timothy," she said in her friendliest fashion. It was part of her scheme to keep him in good humor.

"Mind you bring my daughter home at a reasonable hour," Irene Hastings said with her usual severity.

"Count on that, ma'am," the officer said, bowing again. Then to Diana he said, "Shall we go?"

Diana was anxious to be on the way. A few minutes later they were in a carriage clattering over the cobble-stoned streets on their way to Portman Square and the brilliant social occasion.

Diana sat smiling beside the young officer in the shadowed carriage. Her friend Rose, who was the daughter of the general holding the party, had assured Diana that the man who had won her heart would be among the invited guests. And she had allowed Timothy to escort her on the solemn promise that he would allow her complete freedom to be with the man she loved after they arrived at the great mansion where the party was being held.

Now Timothy reached out in the darkness and tentatively took her hand in his. "Diana," he said, clearing his throat, "may I remind you that I don't like our arrangement at all."

"I won't listen to such talk," she reproved him. "You have made a promise."

"Which I now begin to regret."

"You are an officer. Your word should be your bond."

"And it is! By Jove, it is!" Timothy sputtered. "But I'm thinking of you, of your welfare—and of how your mother would feel if she knew her only daughter had involved herself with a person like Barnabas Collins!"

She turned on him hotly. "And pray, what is wrong with Barnabas?"

Timothy cleared his throat again. "Can't imagine what you see in the fellow!"

"He's charming and handsome. And he has the kind of culture and manners most other young men in London sorely lack!"

The young officer dropped her hand. "Well, that is a bit rough to accept!"

"I'm not talking about you, Timothy," she said quickly to placate him, though he did not measure up to her standards of charm in any sense. "I'm referring to the bulk of the young men in London today."

Timothy said, "I can tell you that Barnabas Collins is a rake, for all his good manners and charm."

"That just isn't true!"

"Upon my word it is!" Timothy solemnly declared as the carriage rattled on. She was sure if she could have clearly seen his round face his expression would have been pained.

"You're speaking with jealousy," she said.

"I'm telling you what the gossip is."

"Gossip rarely interests me."

"You would do well to heed it now," was her companion's advice. "The talk in the city is that Barnabas Collins consorts with theater people, women of ill repute and even criminals. He stalks the streets of London all night long. It is said he never sleeps until the daylight comes."

"It's the way he likes to live," Diana said indignantly. "And why should this make people think less of him? He enjoys the company of theater people and he is always a gentleman where women are concerned. I just don't believe your allegations!"

"I make them on the most solid evidence," the young man at her side said in protest. "Those who know him best claim he is most happy amid the seamy life of the city."

"Barnabas is a kind man. Not a snob like so many of you!"

"There are other stories about him," Timothy went on. "And not pleasant ones. It is said that he, or a man resembling him, has made a habit of attacking young women. A number of them have been found wandering dazed in the streets with ugly red marks on their throats, as if they had been bitten in some fiendish manner."

Diana gave a scoffing laugh. "That is truly a ridiculous accusation."

"It is what I have heard," the young officer said doggedly.

"I don't want to listen to any more such nonsense," Diana told him. "See, we are at the general's house."

The coachmen brought the cab to a halt and they got out. The mansion in Portman Square was alight from top to bottom. Carriages arrived at its door to leave richly clad men and women. Inside, music played and the general and his daughter stood at the head of the receiving line to greet the cream of London society. The guests moved on after this formal greeting to gather in groups in the great living room for wine and conversation, or went directly to the ballroom for dancing. Diana and Captain Grant followed the latter course and joined the dancers.

Diana remained in the young captain's company for a good part of the evening and began to worry when it grew late and Barnabas Collins still hadn't made his appearance. Towards mid-evening she excused herself from Timothy and went up to the balcony to consult Rose.

The dark girl was concerned. "I can't imagine why he hasn't come, Diana," she said. "I personally addressed his invitation."

Diana sighed. "Something may have occurred to prevent his attending. He may even be ill."

Rose studied her seriously. "He means a great deal to you, doesn't he?"

"I love him," Diana said simply.

Her girlfriend glanced down from the balcony to the big hall below. It was filled with chatting couples. Then she touched Diana's arm and said, "Look!"

She followed her friend's glance and was delighted to see that the front door had opened and Barnabas was entering. Erect and handsome in his caped coat, he presented a magnificent figure. The servant took his coat and Barnabas, elegant in a dress suit and white tie, looked up towards the balcony. She waved to him and he smiled at her and started slowly up the broad stairs to join her.

Even though she'd known him for months now and they were in love, she still faced him with a breathless excitement on their every meeting. There was such a magnetism to this tall, dark man. His melancholy, almost cadaverous face, with its high cheekbones and the thick black hair carelessly swept across the intelligent forehead, had a deep meaning for her.

Now he came along the balcony to join her and take her hand. Raising it and touching his lips to it briefly, he smiled, revealing glistening white teeth. "I'm sorry I'm late," he said.

"Just so long as you're here," she told him happily. "I was so afraid you wouldn't come."

Those hypnotic, deep-set black eyes met hers. "I was bound to come, knowing you'd be here."

"I had quite a time getting Mama's permission," she confided. "But when I agreed to let Timothy Grant escort me she allowed me to attend."

Barnabas nodded and smiled thinly. "If I remember correctly, he is the rather stuffy young fellow she wants you to take for a husband."

Diana blushed. Barnabas could make her blush at will. "The same," she said quietly.

He took her arm. "A disquieting thought," he said. "Shall we drive it from our minds by enjoying a dance?"

"Please," she said.

They took their places on the floor for a lovely waltz. Barnabas was a perfect partner and whirled her lightly around the room. She felt she had never enjoyed a better dance. But then, she always felt that way when Barnabas was her partner. At last the music ended, and quite breathless, she allowed him to lead her to one of the quieter side rooms.

Studying her with concern, he asked, "Shouldn't you return to the young captain?"

She shook her head. "It was agreed between us. If I came with him he was to allow me to spend as much time as I wished with you."

Barnabas smiled gravely. "I can't picture the young man enjoying such an arrangement."

"He is an officer and a gentleman," she said firmly. "He must keep his word."

"Let us hope he remembers that," Barnabas said quietly.

Diana looked at him with indignation. "You have no idea how unfairly he talks about you. He tries to make you out some sort of monster!"

"Indeed?" There was a questioning light in the hypnotic black eyes.

"Yes," she said solemnly. "He went on a lot of talk about your roaming around London after midnight and associating with criminals."

"He has a lively imagination," Barnabas observed coolly.

"And he claims some people told him you had attacked several young girls and left ugly marks on their throats."

Barnabas' face took on a strange expression, as if what she'd said had been something he'd heard many times before. In a gentle voice he asked, "And do you believe him?"

"Of course not!" she said. "Let's leave. I don't want to stay any longer. You can take me home."

"What about Captain Timothy Grant?"

Diana shrugged. "I don't see him around. He may have left on his own or found some other girl. I don't think we should wait for him."

Barnabas was waiting at the door for her in his caped coat when she came down in her wrap. He saw her out into the darkness where his carriage was waiting. After giving the address of her home, he got into the carriage beside her.

At once she fell into his arms. He held her tightly and his lips pressed hard on hers for a lasting kiss. She had been in his arms many times before, but she always longed for the moment to be repeated. It seemed that now she was only happy when she was with him. Yet there were some things about him that worried her.

When he released her, she stared up at him through the shadows anxiously. "Are you in good health, dear Barnabas?"

The gaunt face peering at her through the darkness showed small surprise. "Of course. Why do you ask?"

"Your lips. They are so cold. Unnaturally cold."

He smiled. "Don't let it worry you. It's a family trait. You've no doubt noticed my hands are cold as well."

"I have."

"A matter of poor circulation. You needn't be alarmed."

"I'm frightened for you all the time," she said, snuggling close to him. "I want to be near you always. Why can't we be married right away, Barnabas? We could elope."

His arm was around her. "I'd like that," he agreed with a sigh. "But I have a certain problem which must be settled before I think of marriage."

"What sort of problem?"

"Nothing you should concern yourself with," Barnabas told her. "It is something I must work out for myself."

"Will it take long?"

His arm tightened around her. "No longer than I can help," he promised.

"I have a strange feeling," she said unhappily. "I get the idea we won't ever have a life together. That Mama or something else will prevent us marrying."

"You mustn't think such things," he said.

"Will you soon take me to America and your home in Collinsport?" she asked dreamily.

"Yes."

"I have heard so much about Collinwood. I'm looking forward to it."

"You'll find it a good deal quieter than London," he warned her. "It's just a tiny village on the seacoast in Maine."

"But it's where your family live," she said. "Where you belong."

"Yes," he admitted with a sad look. "Where I belong and where I must return."

She studied his handsome profile and in a tone of awed discovery said, "You sound as if you regretted ever leaving Collinwood."

"There are times I do feel that way."

"Why did you leave, then?"

His deep-set eyes fixed on her strangely. "Don't ask me about that," he said in a quiet voice. "Don't ever ask me about that!"

The intensity of his reply startled her. She had come to realize there were times when an invisible curtain came between her and the man she had grown to love. Invisible, but still a barrier that was completely impenetrable. There were things about Barnabas Collins and his past she would never know, that he did not wish her to know. She suspected some unhappy love affair had been the cause of his setting out from his beloved Collinwood. But that was in the past. She had won his heart now. And if he wanted this secrecy she was not going to object.

The carriage rolled on through the almost deserted London streets. She leaned close to him and fervently wished that she could be with him always. At the same time aware the moment of their parting for the night was almost at hand.

The horses were reined abruptly and the carriage halted with a jerk. Diana glanced out the window and saw they had arrived at the entrance to her home. She looked up at Barnabas again with ineffable sadness on her pretty face.

"Take me with you, Barnabas," she whispered.

He gave her a melancholy smile. "Soon," he said. "Be patient." And he kissed her gently.

Barnabas helped her out of the carriage and saw her to the door. They stood in its shadows for a moment in each other's arms. Then he gave her another brief kiss and left her.

She watched his tall, caped figure as he crossed the street and got into the carriage again. In the moment before the driver roused the horses into action Barnabas leaned out the window to wave goodbye. She quickly raised a hand to wave to him in return. Then the coach moved off into the darkness of the London night and was lost to her.

She still remained staring wistfully after it for a few seconds before using the rapper to announce her arrival home. She wondered where Barnabas might be going now? Had he instructed the driver to take him to one of the narrow, squalid streets in the less savory section of the great city? Had he a rendezvous with someone in one of those places where roistering went on all through the night?

She had heard lurid tales of the men and women of that dark underworld with which she'd had no contact. And it seemed unlikely to her that a man of Barnabas' dignity and refinement would lower himself to visit the murky places frequented by the criminal and dissolute. Yet Timothy Grant had insisted this was so.

Still, Timothy was a wildly jealous young man, apt to make any accusation against Barnabas. On the other hand, she knew that Barnabas did have many friends in the theater and never showed himself in his familiar haunts except after nightfall. It represented a puzzling side of his nature, and one that troubled her.

She lifted a dainty hand to use the rapper and then waited for the door to be opened. Only a moment elapsed before one of the elderly maids let her in. Diana smiled at the old woman and crossed the entrance hall on her way to the stairs, but before she'd advanced more than a few feet her mother came out the broad living room entrance to confront her.

Irene Hastings had an angry expression. She said, "So you have come home at last!"

Diana nodded. "I wearied of the party and decided to come home alone."

"A likely story," her mother said, her thin lips curled with disdain.

Diana glanced beyond her mother to see Timothy Grant standing rather awkwardly in the living room. She at once understood everything. With a reproachful look for her mother she moved past her to meet Timothy just inside the door. He seemed uneasy and gave a slight bow.

"What are you doing here?" she asked, although she knew the answer only too well.

"Sorry, Diana," he said stiffly. "I felt your mother should be told about your behavior tonight."

Irene Hastings had come in to join them. Staring angrily at Diana, she said, "Timothy has told me all about you and your friend Barnabas Collins. I will not have you associating with such a man!"

CHAPTER 2

Diana's immediate reaction was one of indignation. Crimson flared up in her cheeks, and facing her mother, she said, "I think there is one important detail Timothy may not have told you. I happen to be in love with Barnabas Collins!"

Irene Hastings looked aghast. "In love with a man who associates with criminals and women of the streets!"

"That is Timothy's story," she retorted hotly. "And it's not true."

"I'm sure Timothy is not given to lies," her mother replied. "And you will do as I say. I order you never to speak to Barnabas Collins again."

"You're asking the impossible," Diana told her, and turning to an unhappy-looking Timothy, she said with contempt, "As for you, Captain Timothy Grant, I want no more of your company!"

"Please, Diana," he begged.

But she had turned her back on both him and her mother and was marching out of the living room to continue on up the stairs. It had been an unpleasant, angry scene and she wanted no more of it. Her mother came sputtering after her but did not follow her up the stairway. After a moment she heard her outraged parent going back to the living room to join Timothy.

Diana opened the door to her own room and went in and

slammed it behind her. Then she leaned against it with tears of humiliation and rage in her lovely blue eyes. Her brief moments of happiness with Barnabas at the gala ball had ended in disaster, thanks to the underhandedness of Timothy. Grim determination replaced her expression of grief as she stood there in the shadowed light of her lamplit bedroom. She had meant what she'd said just now. She was finished with the young captain regardless of what her mother said or did.

All her fears of something interfering with her romance with Barnabas plagued her again. She knew how thorough and merciless her mother could be. And she realized she would have to make a strong fight against her. Once again the prospect of eloping with Barnabas seemed the only wise solution. If she could somehow persuade him that they could be married at once, she would be free of her mother's neurotic tyranny! She must somehow see Barnabas and try to convince him. With this thought, she worriedly began to prepare for bed.

Her night of troubled sleep was followed by a morning of crisis. Any hopes she may have had about avoiding a showdown with her mother over Barnabas were crushed shortly after breakfast. Her mother summoned her to the rear of the great mansion to the tiny room which was referred to as the sewing room.

There, seated primly on a small divan, Irene Hastings sat. She wore a dress of black with a high neck showing only a wisp of lace at the collar. Her once beautiful face was set in grim lines of weariness and annoyance as she greeted Diana. It was apparent she had not spent a restful night either.

Waving Diana briskly to a plain chair with a seat of needlepoint, she said, "We must have a serious talk."

"I don't intend to argue with you, Mama," Diana said plaintively, and she sat in the chair.

"There shall be no argument," her mother said firmly. "You must see that your disgraceful actions are doing me serious physical damage."

"I have no wish to hurt you, but I must listen to my own heart. I do love Barnabas Collins."

Her mother stared at her grimly. "It is possible that you do. But you have a very slight knowledge of the world and the sort of people in it. You know nothing of the character of men like Barnabas Collins. By the account given of him by Timothy, I'd gather that he would only bring you misery."

"Timothy is prejudiced. He's not being fair to Barnabas."

"I have taken that in consideration," her mother said. "But rumors I have heard are too serious to ignore. They say that he spends his nights brawling in taverns and prefers the company of the dissolute to the decent."

"That's not true!" Diana protested. "If you will allow Barnabas to come here you will know it's not! He's a fine gentleman!"

"Pretends to be a fine gentleman!" Irene Hastings said scornfully. "There is a vast difference. This American adventurer knows that you have money and he is after it."

"He loves me!"

"What can such a person know about love? Surely you've also heard that he is suspected of being a debauched criminal? That the London police are watching him! It is thought he is the one making monstrous attacks on young women. There have been at least a dozen instances of such attacks during the past few months. The stories of girls found dazed with weird red marks on their throats have been featured in the press!"

"That's more of Timothy's lies!"

"You must be protected against yourself and against this man," her mother said sternly.

"Won't you please meet him? Judge him for yourself?"

"No. I'll not have a villain like that in this house!"

Diana sighed. "In that case I can only tell you I intend to go on seeing him whenever I can. And I will marry him if he will have me!"

Her mother seemed slightly taken back by the firm manner in which she'd stood up to her. She said, "I've never known you to be in such a rebellious mood before!"

"You have never known me in love before," Diana replied.

"I can see that reason will have no appeal in this matter," her mother said with a trace of weariness showing on her face.

"My pleas that I want only your good won't be listened to."

"I'm afraid not."

Her mother's mood became unexpectedly resigned. "I expected that," she said. "So I have made other plans."

Diana at once was on the alert. "What other plans?"

"I'm taking you away from London and temptation at once."

"I won't leave," Diana protested.

"You will have no choice," her mother said firmly. "And I'm sure a holiday in Italy will do you good. We are to visit the son of one of your late father's dear friends. A titled gendeman."

Diana stood up. "I don't want to visit Italy."

"The arrangements have already been settled," her mother said. "I wrote the Count of Baraga at the family estate in Palermo. I also sent him a pencil sketch of you. He replied at once, begging us to come visit him. He spoke of his loneliness since his father's death and rather pointedly mentioned being a bachelor. I'm sure he was greatly taken with the sketch of you and may even want you to become his

Countess."

Angry tears were in her eyes. "I don't need your matchmaking."

"You should thank me. Consider it! A delightful holiday in Italy. We shall live at the castle of a true count and you may be courted by a romantic young gentleman!"

"I want to remain here and marry Barnabas Collins!"

"That subject is closed," her mother said firmly. "We shall be leaving London for the Continent in the morning. I'll be busy with arrangements for the trip. And I'll expect you to go to work packing your own things. That's the least you can do to help. And let me hear no more about this Barnabas!"

So the unhappy meeting between them ended. After ordering Diana not to leave the house, her mother told her to go up to her room and make preparations for the trip to Italy. Diana went upstairs, filled with frantic thoughts and torments. She had never heard of the Count of Baraga before, though she knew her father had made many friends in Europe. The whole project was distasteful to her.

Dejectedly, she sat by the window of her room which overlooked a small park. It had begun to rain and there was little movement in the street outside. Now and then a fancy carriage would go by and the stout old gentleman in the house next to theirs appeared, carrying an umbrella as he and his giant white bulldog went for their usual morning stroll.

What could she do? She hadn't any doubt that her mother would keep to her promise to leave London in the morning. Diana resolved she would have to wait for her chance to slip from the house during the day and find Barnabas at his lodgings. Surely he would rescue her in this extremity.

With this in mind she half-heartedly went about doing some packing. Her mother came to the room and instructed her as to the bags and trunks she should pack. Diana was more alarmed as it seemed by the amount of luggage they'd be taking her mother expected the visit to be a long one.

A trusted middle-aged maid was ordered to assist her and she suspected the woman had also been warned to watch her and report if she tried to go out. It seemed best for the moment to pretend submission and proceed with the packing as ordered by her parent.

By late afternoon the bulk of the packing was completed. Diana complained she was extremely tired and desirous of having a nap. The maid left her alone and Diana locked the door after her. She hadn't quite made up her mind what to do but knew her mother would also be resting before dinner. It was still raining and unusually dull and forbidding outside.

After a suitable wait she slipped on a flowing dark cape with a hood and quietly made her way out of the room and down a rear stairway that was little used. When she reached the street level she left by a side door and in a moment was hurrying along the sidewalk out of sight of the house.

Bending her head against the rain, she reached a wider and busier street and hoped that she might find an available carriage. She knew the address of the lodgings where Barnabas made his London headquarters and they were some distance from the elegant section where her home was. It was getting dark early with dusk already at hand as she stood shivering in the rain at the busy street corner. She had sufficient money with her to pay for transportation and searched for some approaching vehicle that might be for hire.

Even in this fashionable business street of the old city there were people whose villainous faces made her uneasy. A shabby pockmarked middle-aged man leered at her in an entirely too familiar way as he came by and she quickly turned her head. A moment later two ragged urchins came running across the street and bumped against her, almost sending her tumbling. She clutched her pocketbook, which had been nearly wrenched from her hand by the encounter as the urchins went on their way, howling with glee.

As the darkness increased, her fears grew. She'd about decided to return to the safety of her home when a carriage halted directly in front of her and the driver bent down from his perch with a saucy smile on the battered face under the worn top hat.

"Carriage, miss?"

"Yes," she said gratefully. And she gave him the address of Barnabas. "Can you take me there?"

"Faster than any cab in London," the battered cabby replied instantly. With comic dignity he came down to help her into the dark, musty interior of the carriage.

As he closed the door on her and returned to his perch she felt she'd made an important decision, had faced up to a crisis and won over it. Ignoring the unpleasant atmosphere of the carriage, she sat back as it rattled along the cobblestoned street. The lamplighters had been at work and the gas lamps gave out a ghostly glow that set a tone for all the possible menace concealed by the increasing shadows.

Knowing that the carriage was taking her to the seamy district of the city, she worried about what she would do when she got there. Especially if Barnabas wasn't at home. He had an old and kindly manservant named Peters, whom she'd once met, but she was sure Peters would remember her and be as helpful as he could. However, she deemed it wise to retain the driver and have him wait for her until she discovered whether Barnabas was at his lodgings or not.

When they finally stopped in a narrow back street, she recognized the three-story building in which Barnabas had been living. It was old and sagging. A tiny shop occupied by a tinsmith was on the street level and a flight of rickety stairs led up to the door of Barnabas' quarters on the second floor.

She paid the driver and gave him a generous tip. He responded by doffing his hat in exaggerated politeness. He was quite plainly a character. She asked him, "Will you wait for me? I may need you."

"Depend on it, miss," the cabby said. "I'll not leave this spot until you've given me the word." He glanced up and down the deserted street and bending close to her added, "I'd take care if I were you, miss. Not the most chummy part of town, if you know what I mean. Murder you for half-a-crown, some of the blokes down here!" And he illustrated his meaning more vividly by drawing a finger across his throat to show it being efficiently cut.

"I'll remember," she said in a faint voice and started to leave him to enter the house.

He caught her arm and in another show of confidence whispered hoarsely in her ear, "Just shout if you wants me, miss. Just one little shout and I'll be there! This is the district where that looney has been biting the young gals on the throats and sending them into a fair dazed state. So just you be on the watch! Get me, miss?"

She nodded nervously. "Yes, I get you. Thanks."

She started up the forbidding dark steps anxious to discover if Barnabas was at home. She was beginning to understand her mother's apprehensions about this district of London. It was clear she was taking a chance in coming down to such an area—but she'd been left without choice. She had to talk to Barnabas.

Reaching the top of the stairs, she found herself before a rough wooden door with light seeping out from the wide crack under it. Without hesitation she knocked on the door and waited for an answer. The light inside had given her encouragement, since it suggested that she might have caught Barnabas at home.

She was speculating on the reasons why Barnabas should have chosen such an area for an abode and making up her mind to influence him to move to better quarters at once when she heard a board creak on the other side of the door. Then the door opened slowly and the elderly Peters squinted out at her.

Peters was a little gnome of a man with a completely bald head except for a strange forelock of gray hair which draped across an oddly protruding forehead. "Yes?" he asked in a querulous tone.

"It's Miss Hastings," she told him. "Don't you recognize me? Barnabas entertained me here one evening."

The rheumy blue eyes peered at her. Then a smile of

recognition crossed the little man's face. "Miss Diana! Of course! Now I know you."

She stood awkwardly in the dark hall. "I'd like to see Barnabas."

The stocky old man with the short bow legs made no move to open the door further. "Is he expecting you?"

"No. Not really. But I have to see him."

Peter looked reluctant. "You shouldn't come here unless he says so."

"It's an emergency. Tell him I'm in serious trouble. Will you, Peters?"

The bald man frowned. "It's not usual."

"Please!" she implored him, distressed that she should fail now.

Peters continued to hesitate. "I'll see," he said at last. And he startled her by closing the door in her face and leaving her in the darkness again. She was not receiving a warm reception. Glancing down the shadowed stairs, she hoped the cabby was still waiting for her.

A few minutes more elapsed before she heard swift footsteps inside and the door was thrown open. Barnabas stood revealed with a surprised look on his melancholy yet handsome face. He was wearing his caped coat and apparently ready to go out.

"Diana!" he exclaimed in his sonorous voice. "What are you doing here?"

"I had to see you," she said abjectly. "Something dreadful has happened."

"Come in," he invited her. And took her arm as she entered the small low-ceilinged dining room of the flat. He embraced her, and after a lingering kiss, asked, "What has been going on?"

She quickly explained, including the details of the trip her mother had planned. "She intends to take me to the Continent with her in the morning," Diana said. "I can't leave you."

Barnabas listened seriously, then he said, "Don't worry about that. But you had best go with your mother."

"No! Let's elope tonight! Go off together somewhere she can't find us."

He took her by the arms and, in the same manner he would have used for a frightened child, said quietly, "That's not possible!"

"But if I go with her I may never see you again! She may force me to marry that Count of Baraga! Someone I've never heard of before!"

"You'll not be forced to marry anyone you don't want to," Barnabas told her quietly. "And you'll not be alone. I'll also leave for Italy tomorrow. And I'll be in touch with you as soon as you reach

Palermo."

Diana was relieved at his words though they didn't by any means satisfy her. She said, "But why not let us elope now? Or, barring that, couldn't you present yourself to her and let her discover what a fine man you are?"

Barnabas showed a concerned expression on his gaunt face. "Not yet," he said. "I'm not ready for that."

She was in despair. "But she's not been reasonable about you! Timothy has told her all manner of wild tales about your being a wicked character. She has never met you so she believes them."

He nodded. "I know that. And I will talk to her one day. But this is not the time. You must make the trip to Italy with her and I'll follow."

Diana stared up at him anxiously. "You promise?"

"You have my solemn promise," he said gently. "Surely you understand that our being parted is as unhappy an event for me as it is for you."

"I begin to doubt it," she said, swallowing hard.

"You mustn't," he said earnestly. "Not ever."

Diana gazed into the unfathomable depths of his eyes. "Barnabas, is there some other girl? Are you trying to rid yourself of me so you can give all your attentions to her?"

He shook his head with a sad smile. "You are the one girl I love at this moment," he said. "Please believe that. We can try and settle things with your mother in Italy."

"I'm afraid to go," she said with a tiny shiver. "I have the feeling something awful is going to happen."

"I'll be close to you," Barnabas promised.

"Even so, I'm afraid," she said, pressing against him.

"You mustn't indulge in such unhealthy fantasies," Barnabas reproved her. "It will be all right."

"And you will follow us to Palermo?"

"I've given you my word," Barnabas said. "Now I must get you back to Portman Square safely."

"I have a carriage waiting," she told him. "At least I think it's waiting."

"Good!" Barnabas said in a relieved tone. "I'll take you down to it at once."

"Can't I stay a little?" she asked him in a plaintive voice. "It will be weeks before we see each other again."

His gaunt face showed a mixture of emotions. "I wish I could have you stay," he said. "But I'm expecting a caller. I wouldn't have made the appointment had I known you were coming."

"So I must go?"

"I'm afraid so," he said gently, and with a sad smile he

touched his lips briefly to hers. "Now, let us get you safely on your way."

She allowed him to escort her down the dark, rickety steps. And as they came near the bottom of them there was a loud clamor from outside. Diana was at once alarmed. She had visions of the carriage having gone and there being a riot in the street.

Barnabas left her to dash outside and she followed a few steps after him. The first thing she saw was that the cabby had kept his word. The carriage was still there and he was holding the horse by the bridle and trying to keep it calm in the melee that was going on.

A ragged old woman had come down the street and was being taunted by a band of rowdy urchins. They danced around her and chanted, "Witch! Witch! Old Lena is a witch!"

"Vermin! Street scum!" the old woman screeched at her tormentors, and clawed out at them wildly with scrawny hands. Her long gray hair was crazily askew and the taunting circle kept dancing out of reach.

The wild screaming and chanting kept on. Several of the urchins began hurling stones at the old woman. It was Barnabas who ended the fracas. He bore down on the youngsters and they quickly became silent and dispersed as he came close. He joined the old woman they had been calling a witch and eyed her solicitously.

"Are you all right, Mother Lena?" he inquired.

The crone pushed back strands of the long gray hair from her wrinkled, thin face. "Thank you, Master Barnabas," she said in a reedy voice. "The little beasts were ready to slay me!"

"I'm sorry," he said. "At least they seem to have gone."

Diana saw this was true. The dark street was once again as deserted as when she'd first arrived. Evidently the rowdy youngsters had a healthy respect for Barnabas. It was amazing the way they'd reacted to his showing up. Now Barnabas spoke to the old woman in low tones and led her back to where Diana waited.

"I'm taking Mother Lena upstairs to recover from her ordeal," he told her.

Diana was rather surprised at this but tried to hide her feelings. "It was very unfair of those little ruffians!"

The crone leaned forward, thrusting her wrinkled face close to Diana's. Diana could see the old woman's rotted, yellow fangs and smell the fetid odor of her breath. "Thank you, miss," Mother Lena said in her hoarse croaking voice. "You are a pretty girl and a kind one."

"Thank you," Diana murmured, retreating a little from the filthy ragged creature.

Mother Lena cackled. "Needn't be afraid of me, miss. I can see the future. That's why they hate me. Call me the Witch! And so they may! I can see things before they happen." The glittering, sunken eyes met Diana's. "I can see what's ahead for you!"

"No!" she protested faintly.

"Heat and horror!" the old woman said with a gleeful cackle. "That's what I see waiting for you, miss. Heat and horror! Remember and beware!"

Barnabas quickly intervened. Taking the old woman by the arm, he led her to the door of the old building. "You may go upstairs and wait with Peters," he told her. "I'll join you in a moment."

The crone nodded and paused to point a skinny finger at Diana. "Remember what I said! Heat and horror!" And with a loud cackle of laughter she went inside.

Diana recoiled at this last outburst from the mad old woman. Barnabas came quickly to her with an air of distress. She could tell that he was embarrassed by the crone's behavior.

"You mustn't pay any attention to her, Diana," he said.

She was still suffering from revulsion. Staring up at him in disbelief, she asked, "How can you be so friendly with her?"

Barnabas shrugged. "She's a poor unhappy old thing. I help her whenever I can."

"Is she really able to foresee the future?"

His gaunt face showed a smile. "She thinks so. But you mustn't pay any attention to what she said just now."

"I can't help it. She spoke of heat and horror! Italy will be hot at this season of the year and who knows what horror I may face there?"

Barnabas reproved her. "Now you're allowing your imagination to run wild. Surely you don't believe in witches."

Diana gave him a sharp look. "You two seemed very friendly. And you were quick to rescue her."

"I've explained that," Barnabas said. "Now you must get back to your mother as soon as possible before she has the police at my heels."

She allowed him to see her to the door of the cab, and there she turned to him. "I don't like any of this, Barnabas."

"Nonsense! You mustn't allow a silly old woman to upset you." And he left her to give the driver of the carriage his instructions. Then he bade her goodbye. He stood in the street watching after her and waving as the carriage began the trip back to Diana's home. She studied him through the smoky glass of the rear window until his heroic, caped figure was lost in the darkness. Then she sat back on the horsehair seat with a sigh.

It had been a weird experience, and she couldn't imagine why Barnabas would be on such friendly terms with that wretched old creature of the streets. The children's chanted cries of witch came back to her vividly and made her wonder. Recalling the fairy stories of her childhood, she remembered that often witches were able to change at will into beautiful young women!

Was old Mother Lena adept at this transformation? She might be if she was a real witch. Sitting there in the blackness of the jolting carriage, Diana realized that she was actually exhibiting signs of jealousy of the old woman.

The return to Diana's home made all that had happened in the dark street where Barnabas was living seem distant and unreal. Nervously she paid the carriage driver and then hurried around to the side door to enter the house again. She'd not been gone longer than an hour and a half. If her mother hadn't noticed her absence there would be no need for difficult explanations or more arguments.

With this in mind she climbed the rear stairway, remaining in the shadows, furtive and tense at every sound. It was a lucky time for her. She reached the safety of her room without being seen. And she hoped that no one had been there to find her absent. Quickly she changed into a dress suitable for dinner.

As she braced herself to go down and face her mother she had some lingering thoughts about her meeting with Barnabas. She was badly disappointed in his not agreeing to elope, but she did believe he would journey to Italy to protect her. She had to believe that!

Then the echo of the old woman's shrill words returned to terrify her: "Heat and horror! Heat and horror!" The words beat into her mind. What did it mean? Could Mother Lena really foresee the future. Barnabas had tried to evade the question, but he was plainly impressed by the old woman. Diana could only wonder if he knew a good deal more about the crone's powers than he was admitting, and if some fearful experience was awaiting her in Italy.

CHAPTER 3

Diana's apprehensions were lost in the bustle of last-minute packing and leaving. Timothy came to pay his respects and see her and her mother safely aboard the boat train for France. While her mother went out of her way to be friendly with the mustached young Guardsman, the situation between him and Diana continued to be strained. She nodded to him coldly and kept her back turned to him most of the time.

When they were on the train and he was left behind on the platform, her mother rebuked her for being so cold to him. "He is really very fond of you," she told Diana.

Seated next to her mother, Diana kept her eyes on the train window observing the passing scene. She said, "I'll never forgive him. Not after the way he libeled Barnabas."

"You must forget about Barnabas Collins," her mother said. "We're on the first lap of our long journey to Italy. And I'm positive you will find happiness there. I've been trying to recall what your dear late father said about the old Count of Baraga. As I remember, he pictured him as a handsome, courtly man. I never met him, not having been to Italy before. But I'm sure, judging by his letters, that the young Count will be equally attractive."

"I'm not interested," she said, still avoiding looking at her parent.

"When you meet him you will be," her mother insisted confidently.

And it was in this spirit of optimism that her mother remained all during the warm, arduous train journey from France to Italy. Diana felt far less happy about their adventure. She found the trip endless and she couldn't help wondering about Barnabas and whether he actually was following them such a long way from London.

"The trip has been almost too much for me," Irene Hastings gasped as she weakly fanned herself with a cheap paper fan given her by one of the railway guards. The sun was pouring in through the coach windows which wouldn't open and the heat was nothing less than oppressive. Even Diana felt slightly ill from it.

But she couldn't help feeling sorry when she looked at her mother's pale, perspiring face. "We'll soon be there," she comforted the older woman.

"Yes," her mother gasped. "He will undoubtedly be at the station to greet us. His estate is outside the city. A castle, so he wrote me. I'm sure it will be cool and pleasant there."

"I hope so," Diana said without conviction. She recalled Mother Lena's prediction of heat and horror. The heat they were getting in abundance. Would the horror follow?

"You must look your best," her mother said, giving her an anxious glance. "First impressions are always the most important ones."

Diana smiled bitterly. "The Count of Baraga must accept me as he finds me. And you must get it clearly in your mind that I am not interested in any romantic future with him. I couldn't live here in this hot country."

"It is the time of year. It's probably just as warm in London."

She didn't argue that out with her mother. The older woman sounded so forlorn it didn't seem charitable. And she began to hope that her mother's predictions would come true. At least to the extent that the young count would prove a good host. She worried about the effect of the journey on her mother's health. She would need rest before traveling back to England. The whole thing had been a mistaken venture. She looked grim as she mentally blamed Timothy for bringing it about.

Then the train pulled into the station at Palermo. There was bustle and excitement as the passengers disembarked. Loud male voices shouted orders on the platform in a language Diana couldn't understand. She gave support to her weakened mother and vainly looked around amid the confusion of people and baggage for some sign of the Count. But no one approached them. People either ignored them, brushed by them rudely, or gave them surly stares.

Diana was worried about their bags and trunks, still not unloaded from the train. It was a desperate situation.

She was about to contact one of the railway guards and ask for directions to the British Consulate when she saw a thin, tall man with a neat black mustache come towards them. He was dressed in black and reminded her of a better-class undertaker. Coming up to her, he bowed.

"I am the Count's estate manager, Mario Paulini, and I'm sure you two must be the English ladies he has been expecting."

Irene Hastings spoke up in a faint voice. "Yes, we are. Please do get us and our baggage safely out of here. I'm ill from the trip."

"Of course," the estate manager said suavely. It struck Diana that he had small, hard eyes and they were appraising her very carefully. "First I will get you to the carriage and then I will see about your bags."

With this, he guided them out of the dark hurly-burly of the station into the comparative quiet and sunshine of the street. The carriage was open but did have a top for shade. The estate manager helped them up to the seats and then ordered the sleepy driver to assist him in rounding up their baggage. Irene Hastings, breathless, slumped back on the seat with her eyes closed and her mouth slightly open. Moist beads of perspiration glistened on her pale lined face. Diana, feeling slightly desperate, considered their arrival at Palermo to be something less than auspicious.

When the luggage was loaded and they were jogging along the country road outside Palermo on their way to the castle it became cooler. Diana's mother revived a little and began to take a vague interest in the countryside. Dust rolled up from the creaking wagon wheels and the estate manager, Mario Paulini, sat opposite them in a stiff, ramrod posture, saying nothing unless spoken to. But Diana was again aware of those small, cold eyes studying her.

In spite of the sun and heat she suddenly felt chills of fear. She was certain things were not right, and that her slightly revived parent was in for greater shocks than she'd experienced so far. Diana wished fervently that they could turn the carriage around and flee from this situation into which they were being gradually more involved.

They came to a hilly section of the road. And in spite of the clouds of dust from the slowly turning wheels she got her first glimpse of the Castle of Baraga. It was a noble old building of fine stonework. Its towers and turrets dominated the countryside like some great castle in a fairy tale illustration. The sight of it helped to dispel some of the uneasiness Diana had come to feel.

Her mother gave a slight cry of recognition. "The castle at last! And just as it looked in the Count's photograph."

The thin estate manager's expression was almost one

of arrogance. "Such a castle costs a great deal to keep in repair. Especially when one has expensive and unusual tastes like the Count."

"Indeed," Irene Hastings said with mild interest born of her improved physical state. "Is the Count a collector of art or does his taste run more to farming and improving his lands?"

The estate manager smiled coldly. "You might call Count Baraga an art collector," he observed. "His chief preoccupation is with sculpture. The castle is filled with the most unique examples and there are many figures ordered by him decorating the grounds. You will see them in a moment."

Diana began to feel a little less on edge. Surely a man with the Count's artistic tastes must be all right. And the estate manager, though aloof and peculiar, had been extremely polite and efficient. She mustn't be too quick to condemn.

They passed through a wide gateway with the iron gates open. "Now you will see the Count's statuary," the estate manager said, with what surely was a sneering smile.

The carriage slowed and the dust from its wheels thinned from billowing clouds to almost nothing. And there under the heat of a shimmering midday sun they had their first view of the Count of Baraga's sculptures. Diana involuntarily gave out with a tiny cry of alarm and at the same time she heard a strangled gasp from her mother.

For the scene presented to them was like nothing either of them had ever seen before. Once again Diana was reminded of the prediction of the old woman dubbed a witch back in London. Heat and horror had been her words. And here it was certainly combined.

The carriage rolled on slowly and the estate manager said, "They are rather different, aren't they?"

Diana was too stunned to make a reply. The statuary he was referring to were set out in profusion on the grounds surrounding the castle. Like a ghostly army they stood there, figures which it seemed only a madman could conjure from a demented mind! Heads and bodies of various animals and humans were grotesquely mixed. A huge alligator had the head of a lovely young girl; a bear with a toad's head stood on its hind legs; a horse had the head of a young man; and an eagle ready to take off in flight had the head of a dog. These were only random samples. There were dozens of others, all as perverse and revolting as those she had noted.

There was no beauty in the figures aside from the perfection of their execution. It was as if the Count had ordered the sculptors to make the various creatures as horrible as possible. And they had done excellent work. This garden under the blazing sun with its grotesque monsters was nothing less than a nightmare.

Diana looked at her mother and saw that she bore a stricken look. She said quietly, "Judging from what we see here, the Count must be a most unusual man."

"Yes," her mother said weakly. Glancing at the estate manager with frightened eyes, she asked, "May I inquire as to the reason for the Count's unique collection of sculptures?"

Continuing his disdainful attitude, the thin man in black said, "I suspect it represents a rebellion to the very conservative tastes of his father. In the old Count's day the estate was a showplace of beautiful statuary. But upon his death the present Count of Baraga began to have the fine pieces torn down and these new ones erected in their stead."

Diana's mother gazed at the nightmarish figures dominating the avenues of the large gardens with disbelief. "How many are there?"

"I should say about six hundred," the estate manager said. "Of course I'm not counting those in the castle."

"In the castle!" Irene Hastings gasped with horror showing on her plain face. "He has these fantastic gargoyles in the castle as well?"

The estate manager's cold eyes showed no expression. "Yes. Though some are of a rather different type."

They all lapsed into silence as the carriage neared the front entrance of the castle. Diana studied the statues surrounding the broad lawn and was convinced the Count of Baraga must be mad. Her mother had delivered them into the grasp of a madman! And she prayed fervently that Barnabas Collins had kept his promise to follow them to Italy. It seemed certain they would need help.

The last group of statues were the most insane of all. The Count had made compounds of five or six animals that bore no resemblance to nature. There was the body of a lizard with the legs of a goat and the tail of a fox. The whole thing was weird beyond anything one could imagine.

As the carriage came to a halt the estate manager quickly got out of the carriage and helped them down to the tile walk. After this he spoke in Italian to the sleepy driver, his words addressed in a sharp, biting tone. There could be no question that he was giving the man instructions regarding their luggage. A glance at her mother told Diana that the older woman was trembling in spite of the heat and that she fully realized the dreadful mistake she had made in accepting the Count's invitation.

Mario Paulini seemed somewhat surprised. He told them, "I fully expected the Count would be here to meet you. Something must have detained him. Allow me to show you inside. I'm sure he'll join us in a moment."

He held the door open for them and they stepped inside

to find themselves in a chilly reception hall with not an item of furniture or any decorations on the walls. It had the appearance of a bleak prison cell with a high ceiling. Diana's mother took her arm and leaned on her for support as they went on to a huge living room, where they were presented with another shock.

The great room was furnished lavishly and the floor was of fine marble. Fine tapestries and portraits hung on its walls and two huge crystal chandeliers descended from a ceiling decorated with exquisite tile work and a center mural of a country scene. But their attention was at once taken from these things as they noticed the windows along the length of the living room. They were of a variety of glass of every different color. And there was no pattern to them with blue, red, purple, yellow and green being set together in mad disorder.

And at the end of the room over a fine marble fireplace was a huge clock. To Diana, the clock dominated the area and provided its motif. The clock was cased in a hideous caricature of a Buddha figure. And the eyes of the figure moved with the pendulum, turning white and black alternately and hideously.

As they stood there gazing at it in shocked silence, there was a sudden high-pitched giggle behind them. Diana turned and was further alarmed at the sight of a stooped, shabbily dressed middle-aged man who was regarding them with a simpering smile. But it was his face which she found even more revolting. He looked almost as ugly as the figures on his lawn. His brownish hair was thick and disheveled and his face had a reptilian appearance with his lower lip protruding beyond his upper one, his eyes hooded and menacing and his forehead oddly receding. To cap it all, his skin had an unhealthy, putty-like tone.

He bowed to them and in accented English said, "Welcome to the castle, dear Mrs. Hastings and Miss Hastings." And with almost idiotic haste and no grace he came close and lifted Mrs. Hastings' hand and kissed it. Dropping it hastily, he repeated the action with Diana. Only, this time he lingered over the kiss, his thick, slobbering lips bringing a feeling of true horror to her.

Diana's mother spoke up in a faint voice, "We have never seen anything like the figures in your garden, Count."

The high-pitched giggle came again and the Count rubbed his cheek in a nervous gesture. "I'm glad you enjoyed my little menagerie. I adore them, you know."

Mario Paulini intruded himself between them and their odd host. "I suspect the ladies must be weary from their journey, Count," he said in his cold voice. "They should go directly to their rooms and rest before joining us later for refreshment."

The Count nodded quickly, the dusty brown hair tumbling

over his forehead. "By all means," he said, and giggled again.

"If you will follow me, ladies," the aloof Mario Paulini said, and sedately led them out of the living room and along a dark hallway to a winding flight of grained black marble stairs. Their rooms were joined and on the second floor. The luggage was there awaiting them. After a moment the estate manager left them alone. Diana's mother moaned and collapsed into a nearby chair.

"I'm ill!" she moaned. "What have I done?"

Diana knelt beside her mother's chair. She was frightened but more concerned about her mother's condition, so, hiding her own fears, she said, "I'm sure it will be all right. The Count is eccentric but no doubt quite harmless."

Irene Hastings lay back in the chair with closed eyes. "I wish I could believe that. But everything about this place is so sinister."

Diana sighed. She knew it to be sadly true, but she also knew she must bolster her mother's courage somehow. Her own knowledge that Barnabas Collins would soon be in Palermo gave her strength to carry on. Somehow she must ease her mother's fears.

"We'll feel different when we have rested," she said. "We are both tired from our long journey. And the castle is really beautiful in spite of the Count's macabre taste in art." Rising, she went over to a bust that showed the handsome profile of a man. "At least we have a decent piece of sculpture in this room."

Irene Hastings opened her eyes and stared at the bust set on a pedestal before one of the tall windows. "It is rather nice," she said weakly. And she slowly got out of the chair and went over to examine it. "At least it's not as ugly as the others."

Diana smiled. "It may not be so bad after all."

"Perhaps not," her mother said with resignation, and she moved around to inspect the bust from its other side. At once she drew back with a tiny scream.

Diana joined her and, glancing at the bust, saw what had brought this dismayed reaction from her mother. This side of the bust showed no handsome profile but a grinning skeleton. It was typical of the Count of Baraga's insane taste.

"I didn't know," Diana said with mild despair.

The next several hours were especially difficult for Diana. Her mother had virtually collapsed and refused to countenance any unpacking. Diana pointed out that this was necessary, since they wouldn't be able to get away from the castle for a few days at the best. This brought on one of their bitter arguments which ended with her mother near hysteria stretched out on one of the canopied beds.

Smelling salts and the nervous attentions of a tiny maid, who spoke only Italian but did bring them water for bathing and iced wine for her mother, helped a little. At length the older woman fell into a light sleep. Meanwhile, Diana supervised the needed unpacking and investigated her own room.

In there she found two family statues that had evidently been modeled after some old pictures. The two figures were so strangely lifelike they gave her the feeling of having visitors in her room. The Count had them carved in new and elegant garb of marble. Their shoes were of black marble, their stockings red and the man's suit was of green trimmed with rich, white lace in contrast to the woman's gown of deep blue. The periwig of the man and the headdress of his companion were of fine white. These statues stood one on either side of her bed.

Much as she was disturbed by them and the other examples of fantastic statuary, Diana was more concerned about the ugly Count. And the sinister estate manager struck her as being the one regulating all that went on at the frightening estate. The castle's remoteness from Palermo and the fact neither she or her mother spoke Italian made their position more isolated and desperate. They would have to depend on the good graces of the mad Count and his estate manager to escape.

Could they do that? She hesitated to try to answer that question. She recalled the fact that in his letter the Count had shown a strong interest in her and hinted that he would like to ask her to become his wife. Her poor silly mother had been caught up in this madness in her desire to separate her from Barnabas Collins and the thought that her daughter might be able to marry a title!

Diana smiled grimly to herself as she looked out the window of her room at the macabre creatures of marble in the garden below. Perhaps her mother would agree to her marrying Barnabas now. This dreadful experience would surely teach her a lesson. And again she wondered about Barnabas and when he would arrive. It seemed very likely they would need his assistance to escape the clutches of this madman and his evil servant.

Dinner in the somber dining hall illuminated only by several flickering candles proved another ordeal. The Count's table manners were atrocious. He ate greedily with his fingers and giggled almost constantly. The estate manager sat, taking it all in like an omniscient Satan. In the eerie light of the candles Diana recognized his resemblance to the popular conception of the Devil. But it was only later when they were all gathered in the living room under the hideous clock that she became aware of the worst.

Now the Count of Baraga seated himself opposite her in a high-backed chair and gazed at her with simpering idiocy as the estate manager took a stand between his employer and Diana and her mother.

Gazing at them in his cold fashion, he said, "It would seem

wise that we at once come to the business of your visit here."

Still pale and shaken, but dignified in one of her sedate black gowns, Diana's mother said primly, "The occasion of our visit is not business but to become familiar with your lovely country."

The thin, Satanic face of the estate manager showed a grim smile. "The Count and I interpreted your coming here rather differently. You sent us a drawing of the lovely Signorina which at once caught the interest of my employer. Since he is a very shy man he has asked me to speak for him." He turned to the Count. "Is that not so?"

"Of course! Of course!" The Count of Baraga nodded avidly. "The Signorina is most charming! We shall have a host of children!" And he gave another of his high-pitched giggles.

Irene Hastings spoke up sharply. "I have no intention of allowing my daughter to marry for some time. In any case, she must find a man who can win her heart."

The estate manager's thin face showed disdain. "After she has been here a short time I'm positive the young lady will come to appreciate the Count and be eager to marry him."

"I very much doubt that!" Diana said rising. "And I consider your discussion singularly vulgar and ill-timed!"

"Spirit!" the thin man in dark said approvingly. "I'm glad to see you have it, Signorina Hastings. It is fitting in a woman and a quality needed badly here."

"You must not assume my daughter is going to marry the Count," Irene Hastings said nervously, also getting to her feet.

"I say we should understand what we have in mind and then give the situation a time to develop. The Count offers you his title and this lovely home. Your dowry of beauty and money are most welcome to us. Unfortunately the coffers of the Count's estate have been depleted by his extravagant art expenditures. But the wealth of a rich English wife should soon restore our fortunes here. All in all, it will be an amiable bargain."

The Count of Baraga giggled loudly again and remained in his chair in loutish fashion even though the ladies were standing. His reptilian face showed a sly smile and the hooded eyes regarded Diana greedily. "Beauty and wealth," he said in his high-pitched voice. "And I shall have the money to set out more interesting statues in the rear garden. I have many ideas!"

"You would be wise to forget them," Diana said hotly. "I have no intention of marrying you!" And looking sternly at the estate manager, she told him, "We will want a carriage first thing in the morning. My mother and I will transfer to the hotel in Palermo for the balance of our stay."

The thin man shook his head. "I can't accommodate you in

this matter, Signorina Hastings. I feel you should remain here a little longer. You will find the Count's charms are bound to grow on you."

"I can think of nothing less likely!"

"You have come here to enjoy the countryside," the estate manager said suavely. "So please relax and do just that."

Frustrated and angry, Diana turned to her mother. "Come, Mother," she said. "It is pointless to remain here any longer."

They made their exit to a burst of giggling laughter from the mad Count of Baraga. Humiliated and frightened as she was, Diana was in less of a state than her mother. The older woman seemed on the point of collapse again as they reached the top of the black marble stairway. And when they were in their rooms Diana at once helped her mother into bed.

Irene Hastings gazed up at her from her pillow. "Please forgive me for placing you in this grave peril," she said. "The Count is surely mad and that estate manager is a villain. I don't know what I could have been thinking of when I brought you here."

"We'll find some way to escape," Diana promised her. "Try to rest and don't worry."

"That is impossible," her mother moaned. "And I suddenly realize I am ill. The trip was too much for me. I may never live to see England again."

Diana was shocked. "You mustn't talk like that! I'll ask the estate manager to get you a doctor."

"No!" the sick woman protested. "Don't let him know. He'll only use my illness against us. I'd be afraid of any doctor he'd provide. They might try to poison me!"

"Don't frighten yourself with such thoughts," Diana begged. "When the Count and his manager find I will not consider a marriage, they'll soon let us go."

Her mother stared up at her with concerned eyes. "Don't be so sure! Especially if anything happens to me. They may find evil ways to persuade you. Place you under the influence of drugs or torture you into submission!"

Diana listened to her mother's words with growing horror. A new awareness of the awful position they were in was forced upon her. But she concealed her terror from the sick woman and stayed with her until she fell asleep.

Then Diana went on into her own room and softly closed the door which joined the two rooms. Except for a candle flickering on a table beside her bed, the big room was in darkness. The uneven candlelight cast a glow on the two marble figures carved in such lifelike detail and made them take on an almost living appearance.

She shuddered! What a fantastic nightmare all this was! And yet it was real! That was the terrible part of it. The room was hot and humid and she went over to the big windows and opened them. But no breeze came to cool the room.

Trying to dispel the many fears that beset her, she began to prepare for bed. In the morning she would plead with the cold estate manager to allow them to leave. Perhaps then he would listen to her more kindly. She attempted to make herself believe that. And if they still tried to hold her and her mother prisoner, there was the hope she might attract some attention outside the castle. She would escape the grounds and try to find help. Most importantly, there was Barnabas. He had promised he would come to Palermo and see that she was safe. She believed his promise.

She was standing beside the bed in a thin, white flowing nightgown, reluctant to attempt finding sleep. Suddenly she heard behind her a creaking sound like the turning of a wheel which had not been oiled for a long while. With eyes wide with alarm she turned swiftly to see that a hidden door in the paneled wall had opened and now there was a third lifelike figure in the room with her. Only this one was not carved from stone. It was the grinning Count of Baraga. With a high-pitched giggle he stretched out his powerful hands and came slowly towards her!

CHAPTER 4

Diana cried out in horror as the mad Count moved toward her from the shadows. His lips curled in a lunatic leer as he reached out for her. She deftly moved back to escape the grasp of his outstretched hands, knowing it was only a temporary evasion. The room offered only one exit aside from the hidden door through which the Count had come. And the madman was between her and the door.

Slowly she backed in the direction of the open windows. In her desperation she was considering a leap from one of them if there seemed no other way—even though the drop to the tiled walks far below would mean death or permanent crippling. She would not allow the idiotic Count to touch her.

With another of his high-pitched giggles he came within a few feet of her. She was close against the wall now so that she could feel the velvet of the drapes at her back. The window appeared to be her only hope of eluding him. Then, as she was poised to turn and quickly hurl herself to almost certain death, a completely unexpected turn of events took place.

A weird cry over her shoulder heralded the entrance into the room of a huge black night bird. The fluttering of its wings came close enough for her to feel as it brushed by making its way directly towards the Count of Baraga. Taken by surprise, the madman uttered a frantic yelp and stumbled back. But the huge birdlike creature pursued him relentlessly.

Now the Count was crying out his fear and beating off the sinister great bird. And as a pale Diana leaned against the wall and watched she slowly came to realize this was not a bird but a giant bat!

Her horror of bats had always been basic with her, and this was a monster of the species. Yet she felt no real fear since it had served to defend her. Motionless, she watched the struggle between the giant bat and the madman with fascinated eyes. With a final scream of terror the Count darted behind the hidden door and closed it after him, leaving the bat to bump in frustration against the now-solid wall. After a few seconds it flew back across the room. She involuntarily crouched as it soared in her direction, but the wide wingspread of the frightening creature came nowhere near her. Instead it headed directly for the other open window and flew off into the night uttering a strange, melancholy cry.

Diana gave a deep sigh of relief. And then she thought of her plight and the need to protect herself. Hurrying across the room she took hold of a small but rather heavy chest that sat against the wall and dragged it to a position directly in front of the hidden door. It seemed likely that even the modest weight of the smallish chest would be enough to prevent the door from being used.

As she finished doing this she heard the door to her mother's room being opened and turned to see her mother standing there in her nightgown, looking like a frail phantom.

"What has been happening?" the older woman asked weakly.

Diana at once went over to her. "Nothing you need worry about," she said in a reassuring tone. "You are ill. You must return to bed."

Irene Hastings was not placated. She stared at her daughter anxiously. "I was sure I heard screams and scuffling sounds from in here."

"You may have been having a nightmare. You must return to bed and try and get some rest."

With these words of comfort she managed to get her mother to return to her own room and bed. She promised to leave the door open between their rooms and was glad to do so in view of what had happened. Then she went back to the shadowed silence of her own bedroom. The heat was just as oppressive as before, but there was no hint of the near-violence that had so shortly before taken place there.

A thoughtful expression crossed her pretty face as she

went to one of the windows and looked out. Below, in the park surrounding the castle, the grotesque army of carved monsters were highlighted in the moonlight. She trembled at the memory of her near-escape from the mad Count. And she wondered at the eerie coincidence of the bat flying into the room at just the precise moment of her most dire need. It seemed too provident to have been accidental. And yet it must have been. What other explanation could there be?

The intrusion of the Count and his attempted attack on her had left her in a tortured state of mind. She knew she must get away from the sinister castle as soon as she could. Being burdened with her sick mother, she would find it extremely difficult. She kept remembering the promise Barnabas Collins had made to her and hoped that he would arrive to rescue her. But she couldn't be sure. In the meantime she would again appeal to Signore Paulini and see if he would relent and supply her and her mother with transportation to Palermo. With this thought she went to bed.

In the morning her mother appeared to have some sort of fever. She was much weaker and tossed restlessly in bed. It was apparent that she was too ill to get up and would require a doctor's services. The little Italian maid fussed around trying to be helpful, but the situation was very frustrating.

Diana went down the winding marble stairs and searched through the various rooms of the elegant but strangely decorated mansion until she found Signore Paulini. He was standing on the balcony of one of the smaller rooms smoking a cigar and listlessly studying the array of hideous figures set out among the gardens.

Hearing her come up behind him, he turned and bowed. With a grim expression on his face he indicated the gardens with his cigar and said, "Would you believe that the Count exhausted his fortune having those atrocities committed to marble?"

She ignored his words and told him, "My mother seems very ill."

The estate manager went on regarding the statuary with disgust. "I had to stand by and watch a fortune dribble through his hands."

"My mother needs a doctor," she said in a firmer tone.

The thin face with the tiny mustache, the Satan's face turned to study her. "But things will be better now, Signorina. With you as mistress of the castle there will be money for the required things. All will be well again once you and the Count have married."

Diana faced him indignantly. "I have no intention of marrying your Count. And you must get a doctor for my mother. She is much worse this morning."

The thin man showed interest. "That is too bad, Signorina.

But do not alarm yourself. I shall have a doctor sent for at once."

"Please do," she insisted. "And as soon as my mother is well enough I beg of you to allow us to leave. All we ask is transportation to Palermo."

The estate manager shrugged. "One thing at a time. I will go see about the doctor." And he marched past her out of the room.

Diana watched him go with many misgivings. Had she done the right thing? Would he really get a doctor? More to the point, would he get a good one or some hack who would do his bidding? Perhaps make her mother worse . . . A frightening possibility, but one she would have to risk. Biting her lip in her anxiety, she decided to go back upstairs and remain with her mother.

She was there by the side of the canopied bed when the doctor arrived. All morning the heat had been almost unendurable. And in her mind she kept thinking of Mother Lena's prediction that Italy would offer heat and horror. It had come shockingly true.

The doctor was a short, bowlegged man with a round, moon face and eyes like currants set in a bread pudding. He spoke no English; however, he fussed and prodded over her mother and then spoke to the estate manager in a gabble of words.

To Diana the estate manager explained, "He says your mother has some sort of obscure fever."

"I could tell that myself," Diana said despairingly. "Has he any suggestions for treating her?"

"He is leaving medicine," the estate manager said. "And he says your mother will need careful nursing. She must be closely watched."

"I'll take care of her," Diana said.

"I'll see that you have help," the thin man said.

"There is one other thing," Diana told him hesitantly.

"Yes?" The Satanic face had a mocking look.

"Your employer, the Count, tried to attack me last night. He forced his way into my room by a hidden door. It must not happen again."

"That doesn't sound like Count Baraga. Are you sure you weren't having a nightmare?"

She shook her head. "No. He would have attacked me if I hadn't been rescued by a giant bat."

The estate manager's thin face showed a smile of disbelief. "Now I'm even more certain you were the victim of wild dreams."

Diana blushed in anger. "I'm telling you exactly what happened."

"I would advise you to save your concern for your mother," the estate manager said. "She is the one in danger."

She realized this was true. But she also saw that the thin

man knew all about what had happened the previous night and was not about to offer her help or sympathy. It was entirely possible that the idiotic Count had made the attack on her at the estate manager's bidding. The Count was surely mad, but the estate manager was pure evil!

The doctor and the estate manager left the room together. She resumed her vigil by her mother's bedside. All her other fears were put aside now as the major fear that she might lose her mother became huge and threatening.

The day passed and the medicine left by the odd doctor seemed to have no beneficial effect on Mrs. Hastings. She grew weaker and refused to take any nourishment. She wailed plaintively, "The broth may be poisoned! I don't want it."

It was an impossible situation, and Diana hardly dared to leave the bedside of her ailing parent. The Italian maid came by to do what she could, but she was frightened and unable to understand clearly anything but the simplest instructions. By early evening Mrs. Hastings became less uneasy and seemed to subside into a light sleep.

Diana took a few minutes away from her mother's bedside and was in her own room when the doctor returned. He went over to examine the sick woman and was only there a moment when he turned and studied Diana solemnly with his small, raisin eyes.

He had said nothing but Diana instinctively knew what his grave manner indicated. She ran forward tearfully. "No! It can't be! Mother isn't dead!"

But it was true. The tragedy of her mother's unexpected illness and sudden passing so stunned her that she had little coherent memory of the events immediately following. Both the Count of Baraga and his estate manager showed at least a hint of understanding in the quiet and efficient way in which they managed her mother's burial.

She had a recollection of going downstairs later that evening and discovering her mother resting in state in the great living room. A richly ornamented bronze casket had already been found for her and candles burned at each end of it. As Diana approached the casket in the shadowed room it seemed to her that her mother looked suddenly beautiful again and at peace.

A priest in loose gray cassock and cowl presided at the grave. Her mother was lowered into the ground of the family cemetery at the rear of the castle, mercifully out of sight of the army of monsters in the front gardens.

But the truce between Diana and the Count and Signore Paulini was to be short-lived. The evening after her mother's burial as she strolled sadly in the gardens she was joined by the thin, malevolent manager of the Count's affairs.

Bowing to her as she sat at the edge of a small fountain, he said, "I trust you are feeling better, Signorina."

She raised her eyes to his cruel face. "Well enough to travel. I should like to leave tomorrow."

"That is quite impossible."

"Are you saying you won't let me leave?"

He smiled thinly. "I think it best for your health that you remain. The doctor believes this to be true as well. He has no wish to certify you despite your fantasies. And he thinks a long rest here will cure you."

Diana felt panic well up within her. She jumped to her feet. "What are you saying? Until I am cured of what?"

"The madness no doubt induced by the shock of your mother's death," he said pleasantly. "But you are in good hands. We will take care of you."

"This is preposterous!" she cried. "I'm not mad, as you well know."

He spread his hands. "One does not expect you to be competent to discuss your condition. I can only warn you we have guards placed at all the exits to the garden wall. Any attempt to escape is bound to fail."

"You daren't do this! I'll appeal to the British authorities here!"

"The Count has already written to the Consul and explained about your mother's death and your unhappy condition. He has promised to see you are well looked after and assured the Consul that when you have recovered, the marriage will be carried out. You shall become the Countess of Baraga."

Diana was near hysteria. "Never! I'll kill myself before you force me to marry that madman!"

Dusk was cloaking the garden as the tall thin man regarded her with a mocking smile. "I suspect that after a little time passes you may come to feel differently," he said, and turned and walked back in the direction of the castle.

Alarmed, she watched him go. She was miserably trapped as a result of her mother's lack of prudence. Now alone, she recalled some of her mother's last fears. The warnings that she might be drugged or tortured into submission to the desires of the two evil men who were holding her captive. How easy for them to convince their simple-minded help that the young English signorina was insane! How diabolical of them!

A cry came from the shrouded sky above and she looked up to see what appeared to be a giant night bird. But as she looked more closely at it she began to think it could be a bat. Perhaps the same bat that had rescued her the other night. What a lucky accident that had been!

Thought of rescue made her think of Barnabas. Surely he must be in Italy now if he was coming at all. Perhaps even in Palermo. He would likely check with the British Consul and he would not be fooled by the story of her madness that the Count and his accomplice were circulating. Thought of the man she loved helped ease her panic.

She walked slowly towards the castle, planning to go up to her own room and lock herself in. She was completely alone now and she had to plan her defence as best she could. As she reached the entrance to the reception hall a familiar figure emerged from the shadows to stand in her way. It was the Count.

His eyes held an ugly gleam. With complete abruptness he demanded in his high-pitched voice, "Why don't you want to marry me?"

"Because I don't love you," she said. "Please let me go inside."

"One minute," the Count said, in a manner far removed from his previous giggling idiocy. He was all venom now to match his reptilian countenance. "You should be glad to marry me. And you will be before we finish with you."

Rage swept away any discretion Diana might have had. "I'll die before I marry a wicked, ugly monster like you." She waved to the weird army of statues in the nearly dark garden. "You belong out there with the rest of the grotesques!"

Her outburst seemed to shock him. At least he stood aside a little and she swept by him to hurry up the winding black marble stairway and take refuge in her own room. She'd barely closed the door behind her when she became aware of a figure standing in a distant shadowed comer. The discovery startled her into crying out.

"It's all right," a familiar voice said as Barnabas Collins stepped out of the shadows to take her in his arms.

"Barnabas!" she sobbed brokenly as she rested her head against him. "I was so afraid you wouldn't get here."

"I was delayed slightly," he told her. "I'm sorry about your mother."

She gazed up into his handsome, melancholy face. "You've heard?"

"Yes. The British Consul at Palermo had a message from the Count about her death. It also mentioned your unhappy state of madness."

Diana shook her head, tears still coursing down her cheeks. "The Count is insane and his estate manager is an evil genius. They may have murdered my mother by poisoning her. And they're trying to force me to marry the Count."

"There need be no fear of that," Barnabas said quietly. "I'm taking you out of here at once."

"They have guards all around the place," she warned him. "I can't think how you managed to elude them and get in."

Barnabas was all assurance. "I have my own ways," he said. "But getting you safely out will not be so easy."

"How will we manage?" she asked anxiously.

Barnabas considered. "We won't be able to take any of your things. You can buy what you need later. Peters is waiting with a carriage outside the castle walls. Once we get safely out there, we'll journey through the night until we are a good distance away from the Count and his friends."

She was about to answer him when the door to her room opened and Signore Paulini came in. At the sight of Barnabas, fear and anger showed on his face. He whipped a pistol from an inner pocket and fired directly at Barnabas, but the bullet missed and in the next instant Barnabas had hurled himself on the estate manager.

Diana watched in breathless silence as the two struggled. Barnabas seemed the stronger and in a space of seconds had twisted the pistol from the thin man's grasp. After that it was strictly a battle of strengths and skill. The two rocked in combat and she could see that the estate manager was putting up a desperate defense.

But Barnabas gradually maneuvered him towards one of the open windows. Then he arched the back of his opponent over the balcony until it seemed the thin man's spine would have to snap. The estate manager let out a terrified scream as Barnabas edged him over the balcony a slight bit further and he fell, wildly flailing the empty air to land in a crumpled heap on the tiles far below.

There was an eerie silence as Barnabas turned to her and in a low voice said urgently, "Let us be on our way."

She allowed the powerful Barnabas to lead her out of the room and down the wide black marble stairway. There seemed to be no one in sight as they went through the hall and out into the gardens. But they'd only gone a few steps when a voice called out to them.

"Halt!" It was the Count of Baraga, with a gun pointed straight at Barnabas' heart. Scowling, the Count said, "Let her go and leave here at once or I'll kill you."

"You are a fool!" Barnabas said with contempt and stood facing the gun muzzle with no apparent fear.

"You were warned!" the Count cried in his high-pitched voice, and to Diana's horror, fired the gun. The bullet had to hit

Barnabas in a vital spot. But to her amazement, its impact did no more than make him stagger slightly.

"I told you that you were a fool," he said in a low voice and moved slowly towards the Count.

The reptilian face of the castle's owner was a mask of astonishment. Horrified astonishment! His mouth gaped open and he held the gun limply, seemingly incapable of firing again.

Barnabas grasped him in his powerful hands and a struggle much like the one that had taken place in the room began. But the Count was no match for the powerful Barnabas. Diana watched as the man she loved threw the Count down. The Count lay there limply, and as he began to stir like a reviving viper, Barnabas did an astounding thing.

One of the more revolting of the statues stood nearby, a goose with a fox head. Barnabas seized the piece of sculpture from its marble mount and hurled it down on the prostrate body of the Count. It was like someone grinding down a squirming snake with a huge boulder and had the same result. The Count was crushed under the impact of the heavy statue and lay there motionless. He had to be dead!

Barnabas came back to her and taking her arm guided her down an alley between the rows of sculptured horrors. "Get away at once," he gasped. "Our best chance."

"The bullet," she said. "Are you badly hurt?"

"Not hurt at all."

She thought he was merely saying this, because she had seen him stagger when it struck him. But he was showing no sign of being hurt now.

They reached one of the gates, and just as the estate manager had warned, there was a man standing guard. Barnabas made a motion for her to wait and be silent. Then he moved forward in the growing darkness and before the guard knew what was happening Barnabas had stalked him from behind and his powerful hands were around his throat. The guard didn't utter a sound but sank unconscious beneath the strangling grip.

Then Barnabas came to her and they hurried out through the gate together. A short distance down the road, Peters was waiting for them with a big carriage. In a moment Diana was safely inside it with Barnabas sitting with her. His arm went around her as the carriage got under way.

"It will be all right now," Barnabas promised her.

They journeyed along narrow dirt roads and through macabre wooded areas until it was close to dawn. Then the carriage halted before a tiny inn at the edge of a small town. Barnabas helped her down from the carriage and escorted her inside. A sleepy inn owner guided her and Barnabas to her room.

At the door he kissed her goodnight and said, "You must be exhausted. Try to get some rest. We'll talk and make our plans tomorrow."

She looked up into his melancholy, handsome face with alarm. "Your wound. You must have it looked after."

He nodded. "Don't worry. I'll take care of it."

And so they parted for the night. She was so completely weary that sleep came with an amazing rapidity. It seemed hardly any time until she opened her eyes to the late morning sun. A maid brought her breakfast and when she had dressed she went in search of Barnabas. She didn't find him but instead was greeted by the faithful Peters in the yard outside the inn.

The little man with the bald head bowed to her. "I trust you are recovered from your dreadful experience, Miss Hastings."

She smiled wanly. "It will take more than a few hours to do that, Peters. But I do feel much better. Where is Barnabas?"

The gnome-like Peters hesitated. "He had to seek treatment for his bullet wound. But he will return at dusk."

Alarm crossed her pretty face. "I was afraid it might be serious."

"It's nothing to be upset about, miss," Peters said earnestly. "But the master felt he should have it given proper attention. You will do best to rest during the day. It is the plan to ride to the nearby seaport of San Mariana tonight."

"I see," she said, with some relief on being told that Barnabas was in no danger from the injury. "Barnabas appears to favor travel by night."

The little gnome of a man nodded with a rather strange, wise look on his lined face. "That is quite true, Miss Hastings. In time you will become familiar with his customs."

Diana tried to put aside her worries about the man she loved, and she followed the advice given her by Peters and went to her room during the afternoon. Sleep came readily and she wakened in time for dinner, feeling much refreshed. She had dinner alone before the hearth in the main room of the small inn. And as twilight came she began to be restive for Barnabas to return. She found her fears for his health mounting.

Dusk had settled as she went outside to find Peters and instead encountered Barnabas standing by the carriage giving his elderly servant final instructions regarding the drive. He turned to greet Diana with a smile.

"Well, are you ready for another long ride?" he asked.

She looked at him with troubled eyes. "Are you all right now?"

"There is no reason to concern yourself," Barnabas said. "It was only a minor flesh wound. The doctor looked after it. What about you?"

"I've spent all day resting," she said. "But wouldn't it be better to travel during the daylight hours? I think we should make much better time."

Barnabas studied her thoughtfully. "It is cooler at night. And I also have another personal reason for preferring night travel."

"You are the one to decide," she said. "Peters told me we were going to San Mariana."

"Yes," Barnabas agreed with a faint smile. "There is a ship waiting there for us. A ship that will transport us across the Atlantic to America. You will soon be seeing the Collinwood I have told you so much about."

She looked up at him happily. "It's what I've wanted so long. But I have no clothes. My bank in London must be informed about what has happened, and also about mother's death."

"There will be time in San Mariana for that," he assured her. "It is a fairly large city. There are some interesting shops there. And a gentleman and his daughter will be joining us there. I have a slight acquaintance with him and he is coming to America to work on an experiment. He will be taking a house in Collinsport not far from Collinwood. His name is Dr. Rudolf Padrel and he will have his daughter Maria with him. She will be company for you during the long voyage and when you reach Collinsport as well."

"That will be very nice," she said.

"You will like Maria," Barnabas said solemnly. "She is a lovely girl. But despite her father's famed talents as an alchemist he has been unable to cure the consumption which is rapidly draining her of health. I fear she has not long to live."

"How terrible for her!"

"She has learned to accept it," Barnabas assured her. "She is a bright, gentle person, who rarely refers to her malady. It would be well for you to follow her example unless she mentions it."

"I understand," Diana said. Then, looking shyly at Barnabas, she continued, "There is one other thing. Shall we be married before we go to America or after we get there? I'm sure Mother would not object to our marrying at once, knowing that you rescued me from that evil castle."

Barnabas frowned. "That presents a matter of the utmost importance," he said. "I feel the time has come for complete frankness between us."

"Yes?" she questioned him, not knowing what he meant.

His deep-set, black eyes met hers. "I love you a great deal,

Diana. But I must be truthful with you. Follow me into the inn."

She did and he took her down the narrow dark corridor leading to the various rooms. He halted before the one that had been his for the night. His hand on the doorknob, he said, "I want you to prepare yourself for a great shock."

"What is it, Barnabas?" she asked, mystified.

He made no reply but opened the door and waited for her to go in. She moved slowly toward the open doorway and stared inside at the shadowed room. What she saw made her gasp, for there on the floor was an open coffin, quite empty, with a burning candle at its head.

CHAPTER 5

As Diana stood there gazing at the coffin with startled eyes Barnabas shut the door after them so they could not be heard outside the room. He moved closer to her. There was a strange expression on his gaunt face that made her feel certain he was about to reveal something of overwhelming importance.

"Does this coffin upset you?" he asked quietly. "Have you a fear of the dead?"

She studied him and tried to fathom what he was attempting to tell her. "It is a strange thing to find in your room," she said. "What does it mean?"

"In telling you, I will risk your turning from me," he warned her.

"That is not likely to happen."

There was a moment of silence in the eerie atmosphere of the shadowed room. The candle by the head of the coffin offered a feeble, flickering glow. The empty coffin was like a grim question mark. Why was it there? Who was it for?

Barnabas' face was solemn. "The coffin is mine."

"Yours?"

He nodded gravely. "Yes. It is where I spend the days from dawn to dusk."

"But why?"

"It's a long story," he said. "I'll make it brief by telling you I bear a curse. A curse that has turned me into an exile and a fugitive. I am one of the living dead."

She felt vaguely faint. "One of the living dead?"

"I'm tainted by the vampire curse. It was put on me many years ago. Since then I have wandered, caught between life and death. Occasionally I must forage for innocent blood to keep myself alive."

It was not like anything she expected to hear and she listened in stunned confusion. She confessed, "I'm not sure that I understand you. Who placed this curse on you?"

His expression was sad as he stared down at the coffin. "A beauty from the West Indies named Angelique. It happened long before you were born. I still bear her curse."

"Is there no hope of a cure?"

"At last I have a slight hope," Barnabas told her. "The Dr. Padrel I mentioned, who will join us in our journey back to America, is an alchemist of repute. He has been working on a serum to cure conditions like mine. And he plans to carry out some experiments on me. With luck I may be able to resume my life as a normal man in a few months."

"Oh, I hope so, Barnabas," she said, taking his hands in hers.

He stared at her in surprise. "You're not afraid of me? You don't hate me? The chill of my hands and lips don't cause revulsion in you?"

"Not when I understand," she said with sincerity. "I know what a fine person you are, Barnabas. And I can't forget that you saved my life. It also happens that I love you. So why should I fear you?"

The tall, handsome man eyed her with admiration. "I never hoped to win a love like yours. And I promise you I'll try to be worthy of it."

"I'm trying to understand," Diana said, and she glanced at the coffin again. "It is because you must remain in your coffin during the daylight hours that you have been unable to travel at those times?"

"Yes. In the coffin there is earth from my grave in Maine. I must never be without it. Until I am cured I'm chained to the coffin during the daylight hours."

"And you keep Peters to protect you while you sleep in the coffin?"

"Yes."

She smiled at him. "Now you'll have the two of us. And you must ask your professor friend to work quickly to remove the curse."

"I think he will succeed this time," Barnabas told her. "He tried once before and failed. But he has come up with some new potion. And I will not risk a marriage with you until we are safely at Collinwood and I have my health."

"I'm willing to become your bride now."

His smile was sad. "The bride of a dead man! No, my dear." And he drew her to him and kissed her tenderly but briefly. "We must be on our way. I will have Peters lash the coffin to the rear of the carriage. It was only because of your upset state that you missed noticing it there last night."

Her pretty face took on a shadow. "I must try to forget that awful castle and the terrible things that happened to me there. I feared I would lose my reason."

"It's safely behind you. They will trouble you no more."

"Poor Mother!" Diana said sadly. "She found out her error too late. And it cost her dearly!"

Barnabas moved toward the door and held it open, all buoyant assurance now that this was settled between them. "You are going to forget the past and so am I. At the port of San Mariana a schooner is waiting for us. It will take us to Collinwood and a new life."

Diana was caught up in his optimism. She carefully shut her mind to the fact he was a living dead man, though it explained why the bullet had not hurt him. He was a phantom, with only a frail grasp on the life he had once known. But she was sure he could be cured and they would find happiness as man and wife. And she had high hopes that the alchemist Dr. Rudolf Padrel would be the one to help him.

These hopes continued after she had arrived in the small Italian seaport and had met the strange doctor. She spent a day purchasing a new wardrobe and in session with the British Consul at San Mariana. He promised to forward her messages to London notifying her solicitors of her mother's death and advising them to settle the legal affairs of the estate. She gave her address as Collinsport in Maine. These important matters looked after, she boarded the large schooner and was introduced to Dr. Rudolf Padrel and his daughter Maria.

Maria was a charming girl with a frail air about her, but no one ignorant of her being a consumptive would have guessed that her hold on life was tenuous. She had shining black hair, large green eyes and a ready smile. The only hint of her condition was that she seemed to tire readily. Her father was as ugly and ungainly as she was pretty and graceful. Diana was struck by the contrast between the two.

Dr. Padrel had been on deck when she went aboard the

ship and at once had come forward to shake her hand. He was a wizened, short man with a head out of proportion to his body. His head was immense! And the fact that he was bald, completely bald, and that his head had a strange flat top made him seem as grotesque as some of the Count of Baraga's mad sculptures. His eyes were large and solemn and of a pale blue tint. To complete his bizarre appearance he wore thick-lensed glasses in square frames.

"Miss Hastings," he said with a slight guttural accent. "Mr. Collins has spoken of you so much that I have been eagerly waiting to meet you."

"And I have been anxious to meet you," she said. "Everything depends on your help."

Dr. Padrel blinked behind the square glasses. "Yes. The experiment. You need not fear, dear lady. This time I am confident of success."

"Is it possible to begin treating Barnabas before we arrive in America?" she suggested. "Couldn't you start the work while we're on shipboard?"

The man with the big head smiled sadly. "That would be impossible. The equipment I use in distilling the various chemicals in my new process is much too complicated to install on the ship. It must wait until I reach the house Mr. Collins has leased for me in Collinsport."

"I see," Diana said with a trace of worry in her voice. She had liked Maria Padrel, but there was something about the father that made her uneasy. Was there the suggestion of crafty pretense about him?

It bothered her all during the long voyage to Boston. Through the daylight hours Barnabas remained in his cabin in the coffin he had shown her. This meant she was thrown much in the company of Dr. Padrel and Maria. Her only other companion on the voyage was Peters. She admired the old man's loyalty to Barnabas.

One day when they were nearing the end of the voyage she came upon Peters leaning against the railing at the bow of the ship. The weather was fine and the sea calm. She joined the old man in gazing at the billowing waves as the fine ship moved easily along.

"We will soon be in America," she said.

Peters turned to her with a smile on his lined face. "Yes, Miss Hastings."

"I wonder about Maria," she said. "She seems very fond of Barnabas. Do you think she properly understands that he and I are soon to announce our engagement?"

"I doubt it," the little man said. "Mr. Collins is kind to her because he knows she has only a short time to five."

Diana sighed. "Yet she seems as well as any of us."

"The consumption can be a deceiving ailment," he reminded her. "Her father assured Mr. Collins that it was unlikely his daughter would see the year out."

"That is distressing!"

"Yes, miss. So if the master appears unduly attentive to Miss Padrel, there is a reason for it."

"I know Barnabas is a very kind man," she agreed. "What is your opinion of Dr. Padrel? I mean, of his ability? Especially his ability to help Barnabas."

Peters rubbed a hand over his bald pate. "It is hard for me to say. I'm not a learned person like the doctor."

"Still you must have a feeling about him," she persisted.

Peters frowned. "Well, if I met him as a stranger I don't think I'd like him. But, knowing him to be a fine specialist and ready to help my master, I'm bound to accept him."

"Are you positive he can aid Barnabas? What is his reputation based on?"

"I'm sure I can't reply to that," Peters said. "But you might ask Mr. Collins. He'd know."

So Diana waited until that evening when Barnabas appeared. It was a lovely moonlight night with the ocean as calm as glass. Barnabas walked along the deserted upper deck with her, seeming oddly aloof and vague. She also thought he was very pale and wondered if it was an illusion caused by the eerie silver of the moon.

They came to a halt amidships and she looked up into his face. "You look very weary and strained tonight," she said.

He stared at her. "Why do you say that?" he asked in a taut voice.

"It's in your face. You don't seem yourself."

"Perhaps I'm nervous because it is nearing the end of the voyage. I'm anxious to get to Collinsport and have Dr. Padrel begin his experiments."

"He's an unusual man," she said. "You have great faith that he will help you. Has he been successful in treating others with the vampire curse?"

The deep-set eyes of Barnabas bored into hers. "If any man can help me, it is Dr. Padrel."

"But what are his credits? His proof of his abilities?"

Barnabas laughed harshly. "In the field of the supernatural there are no proofs. A man like Dr. Padrel offers no credentials. One either accepts or rejects him on the basis of faith."

"And you have faith in him?"

Barnabas clenched his silver-headed cane in his hand. "I

must have faith in someone. I cannot wander on through the years as I am." The real desperation in his voice was touching.

"I'm sorry," she said. "I didn't mean to suggest he was a charlatan. I only wanted to try and find out something more about him."

"He does not like to talk about himself," Barnabas said, and Diana saw that he was actually trembling. She had never seen him in a mood like this before.

"You seem very unwell," she said. "You're trembling."

"I'm sorry," he said, looking out across the ocean. "Perhaps you had better retire. I need to be alone. I have many things to consider."

Diana was surprised and hurt by his suggestion. Normally he begged her to stay up with him as long as possible. Now he actually seemed to want to be rid of her.

"Very well," she said in a small voice. "Good night, Barnabas." And she waited for him to kiss her. Instead he merely turned his back on her and waited for her to leave.

Hurt by his actions, she descended to the lower deck and went down to her cabin. She had been unable to understand his behavior. She had not turned against him when he'd revealed himself as a vampire. She was accompanying him to America and willing to wait until he was treated before their engagement was announced. Yet tonight he had been cold to her. Was he turning from her to the charms of the black-haired Maria?

This troubled her so much she was unable to think of sleeping. After a little she decided to go up on deck alone. Perhaps by now Barnabas might have recovered from his strange spell and be feeling better. With this in mind she made her way back to the main deck. She'd barely emerged into the open when she saw a strange sight in the stern of the vessel.

Maria was standing there alone with Barnabas approaching her unseen. As he came close to her he took hold of her shoulders from behind and drew her to him. At the same time he bent close to her as if kissing her neck. But there was a strangeness about the kiss, a kind of fierce intensity to it. And Barnabas kept his lips to the girl's throat for an unseemly long time. Diana, in the shadow of a lifeboat, watched from her place of concealment with shock and incredulity.

What did it mean?

After what seemed an endless time Barnabas let the girl go and turned and walked rapidly away from her. Diana was terrified that he might come by where she was standing and discover her, but he didn't. Instead he climbed up to the deck above. But she did get a glimpse of his face at fairly close range and saw that the taut look had vanished from it. He appeared actually refreshed.

She turned her attention to Maria and saw the girl slowly making her way back along the deck, yet she appeared to be in a dream state. Her demeanor was that of a sleepwalker, and she walked directly by Diana without even noticing her. Diana had a hard time stifling a gasp, for as the frail dark girl went by she saw a smear of blood on her throat. And the bloody spot was where Barnabas had kissed her!

Diana stood there rigid for long seconds. Her mind went back to the fearful moment at the inn when Barnabas had revealed the truth about himself. And he'd explained that as a vampire he regularly lusted for blood. That he had to feed on the blood of the living to sustain himself. It was part of the curse. And in a flash she understood. Barnabas was preying on Maria for the blood he so urgently required. That was why he'd been in such a nervous mood and insisted that she leave. He hadn't wanted her to find him attacking Maria. It was macabre.

She could only hope his feasting on the frail girl for her blood would do her no harm. And it apparently didn't, for when she joined Maria on the deck the following morning the black-haired girl seemed her normal self. But Diana's sharp eyes did catch a glimpse of the red mark still showing on the other girl's slender throat.

Seating herself by Maria, she asked, "Did you sleep well last night?"

Maria nodded brightly. "Yes. Though I did have a most vivid dream."

"Oh?" Diana waited to hear what it might be.

Maria blushed. "It's rather silly."

"Please tell me," she begged. "There is so little to entertain us on the voyage that even the smallest bit of gossip helps."

Maria's large green eyes twinkled. "You must never repeat what I say to anyone. Especially to Barnabas."

"Of course not."

"I had a dream that I was walking on deck, and Barnabas came and kissed me. It was a strange, lingering kiss that left me in a blissful daze. When I looked around he had gone without a word. Of course, I woke up in my own bed to realize not any of it had happened."

"How odd!" Diana smiled. She knew it was best to keep the truth from the girl. Best for Maria as well as Barnabas. She was going to ask her some more questions, but her father came strolling along the deck to join them.

Dr. Padrel was wearing a cap which emphasized the size of his head in comparison to his body and made him appear slightly ridiculous. He bowed to Diana.

"The captain reports we shall see shore in the morning," he announced. "And we shall dock at Boston in the afternoon. Then it will be simply a short trip in the coastal night boat that plies between Boston and Bar Harbor. We should reach Collinsport in the early hours before dawn."

"I'm sure we'll all be glad to get there," Diana said.

"Indeed I shall," Maria agreed. "I look forward to our new home."

Dr. Padrel's pale blue eyes had a gleam as he said, "Most importantly, I want to begin my treatment of Mr. Collins."

"I hope you won't lose any time," Diana said.

He shrugged. "It will depend on what has arrived for me to work with. There are certain ingredients I have ordered and must have before I can initiate the first steps in the experiment."

Diana wondered if the statement might herald a host of excuses for delays on the doctor's part. She hoped not. She was counting on the powerful alchemy of Dr. Padrel to cure Barnabas almost as much as Barnabas himself counted on it. She couldn't bear to think of failure any more.

That last night of the voyage Barnabas was a changed man, entirely different from the trembling impatient who had ordered her to retire the night before. It was evident that the feast of blood had done him great good. He talked enthusiastically of Collinsport and the arrangements he had made for them all.

"You will be staying in the new Collinwood," he informed her. "You are to be the guest of my cousin Stephen and his wife Maude. They have three sons, the oldest being Jim, in his twenties. He is learning the fishpacking business with his father."

"And where will you be?"

He smiled. "I'm taking up residence in the old house. I spent some time there two years ago. It is still in very good shape and Peters will take care of the household duties." He gave her a meaningful glance. "You understand why I must have my privacy."

"I do," she said with a sigh. "And I trust all that will end when Dr. Padrel begins treating you. Where will he be living?"

"My cousin has leased him a fine house near Collinwood. It is located directly on the cliff overlooking Collinsport Bay. And it has a most unusual feature. Its owner, fearing robbers, had a secret escape tunnel dug from its cellars to the face of the cliff. The opening on the cliff side is high above the rocky beach and offers an avenue of escape only if one had a sturdy length of rope or a rope ladder of the same type. The builder has long since died and I don't think the cave was ever used."

"It's a strange story," she said.

Barnabas smiled faintly. "Collinsport can boast of many strange stories."

The next afternoon they docked in Boston. No attempt was made to leave the schooner until dusk. Then Barnabas emerged from his cabin to supervise the move. They had only a short distance to travel to reach the wharf where the night boat was under steam and about ready to depart. Their luggage was loaded aboard, including the coffin used by Barnabas. Diana noted that Peters had discreetly camouflaged the casket by covering it with canvas. Still, it had a suggestive look.

They were all filled with excitement as the coastal sidewheeler swung out of Boston harbor on her way to Maine. Diana and Barnabas spent most of the night talking. The others had found places to settle down and sleep for the long night trip, but Barnabas held Diana's interest and kept her awake with tales of Joshua Collins and his several sons.

At last, an hour or so before dawn, they docked at Collinsport. Barnabas led her up the gangplank onto the wharf. A fairly large group of villagers, mostly men, were gathered to see the night boat in. Dockworkers loaded and unloaded cargo and there was much shouting and confusion. Diana was quick to see that some of the village men recognized Barnabas and it seemed to her it was a hostile recognition. They looked more sullen and uneasy than pleased at the sight of the tall, handsome man in the caped coat.

Barnabas paid no attention to them at all but sought out a bronzed, attractive young man with corn-colored hair who stood near a wagon with a pair of matched grays.

"That is Stephen's son Jim," he informed her. "He is here to meet us and take us to Collinwood."

When the young man saw them he came forward and said politely, "So you have returned, Uncle Barnabas."

"Yes. I assume your father is expecting me," Barnabas said.

The youth nodded. "The old house is ready."

"Fine," Barnabas said. "This is my fiancee, Miss Diana Hastings."

Jim Collins smiled faintly for the first time. "Welcome, Miss Hastings," he said. "My mother has your room ready in the main house."

"I trust I'm not imposing," she said.

"Mother enjoys company. Especially anyone from a great city like London," Jim replied pleasantly. "I warn you she'll plague you with questions."

"And I shall try to answer them," she laughed.

Barnabas asked the youth, "Is the cliff house ready for Dr.

Padrel?"

"Yes," he nodded. "And a heap of things have come ahead for him. Most of them boxes from New York."

"That is laboratory equipment he has been expecting. I assume you have taken good care of them."

Jim looked sullen. "I had them put in the cliff house as I was told to."

"Then that is all right," Barnabas said. Glancing toward the torchlit wharf he said, "We had better go sort out our luggage and get the doctor and his daughter."

That was the scene that marked her arrival at the rambling big house called Collinwood. Diana had heard so much about it she felt she knew it from its deep, dark cellars to its ghostly chimneys streaking up to the sky. And Stephen and Maude Collins were exceptionally kind in their welcome. Jim was the eldest son with the other boys not yet in their teens, so it was Jim she saw the most of.

And she was embarrassed to note that he seemed to have taken a boyish fancy to her. He kept staring at her and he was always at hand to do any small service she might require. Since she was about to become engaged to Barnabas she found this awkward. She didn't want to hurt the nice young man or his parents. But she knew that if she was to stay on in the great forty-room house she would have to find a way of handling the situation.

From her window at Collinwood she could see the stately white house where Dr. Padrel had taken up residence. It could hardly be more than ten minutes walk away if one used the path along the beach. And Barnabas was in the old house located between Collinwood and the cemetery. She had walked back past the outbuildings to study the old building. It was smaller than the new Collinwood but was of stone and must have been impressive in its time.

Peters came out to greet her in a happy mood. "The master is glad to be back," he confided in her as they stood on the steps. "This was his home at one time and so it means a great deal to him."

"Is it still in good repair?" she asked.

"It did run down badly for a time," the little man said. "But two years ago Mr. Stephen Collins had it restored. You can come in and see the living room if you like."

She entered the cool hallway of the gray building and followed Peters to get a view of the living room through a wide doorway. It was richly furnished and had a fine fireplace. She could easily picture Barnabas playing the role of country gentleman in these surroundings.

"I hope the doctor cures him and he is able to remain here," she said.

The bald man nodded. "Yes, miss," he said quietly.

"Where is Barnabas now?"

Peters appeared uneasy. Then he said, "In the cellar, miss. There is a room he has specially prepared for his use in the day."

"I understand," she said quietly as she had a mental picture of Barnabas down there in his coffin. The horror of it tormented her and she prayed that Dr. Padrel would save him.

She remained to talk with Peters a few minutes longer and then went back to the house. At dinner Maude Collins, who was a gregarious woman, asked her interminable questions about the London fashions. Stephen, her husband, was a stern, gray-haired man with little to say. But Jim often gave Diana an amused glance, as if to remind her that he'd warned her how things would be. The two younger boys remained freckled enigmas who peered at her over the table and giggled surreptitiously.

After dinner, Jim suggested that he show her Widows' Hill. "It's one of the loveliest spots around even if there is a gruesome legend attached to it," he said. "And there's a fine sunset tonight."

Diana would have preferred to wait and go there with Barnabas when he appeared, but she didn't want to be too abrupt with the youth so she agreed to go with him. He was as handsome as Barnabas in a different, younger way and had a good share of the Collins charm. His talk was general as they made their way along the cliff to the high point known as Widows' Hill.

There he halted to point out the various landmarks: Collinsport village and Collinsport lighthouse on the point jutting far out to the ocean. After he'd acted as guide he turned to stare at her with a strange intensity.

"Why are you going to marry Barnabas?" he asked with incredible bluntness.

She blushed. "What makes you ask such a question?"

"I can't help wondering. You are so nice. And sensible."

"Your Uncle Barnabas is a fine man," she pointed out.

His face took on a meaningful expression. "Folks around here aren't as sure of that as you seem to be."

She frowned. "What do you mean?"

"He was here for a few months two years ago," the youth went on. "A lot of strange things happened. Things the villagers blamed him for. At the end Barnabas left in a hurry one night. My father hoped he wouldn't return."

"Yet he welcomed him?"

"Not a welcome," Jim Collins assured her with youthful earnestness, "he just put up with his coming back because he is a cousin and he can't very well turn him away."

"Why should people feel as they do about Barnabas?"

Jim eyed her shrewdly. "Don't you ever wonder what he does in the daytime? No one ever sees him until dusk. And he disappears before dawn."

"He is a night person and unwell," she lied valiantly for the man she loved, hoping it would help. "He is counting on Dr. Padrel to cure him of his restlessness at night so he may live a normal life."

The blond young man looked skeptical. "That may be what he told you," he said. "But people here remember that the first Barnabas Collins was supposed to be a vampire. And they think maybe this Barnabas is one as well."

CHAPTER 6

Diana stood in the sunset glow of the hill in shocked silence for a moment. Jim Collins' unrelenting eyes never moved from her. It was as if he were trying to penetrate her mind and read her thoughts. She felt naked and defenseless before him.

At last she managed, "That's a mad thing to say!"

"Maybe and maybe not," was the young man's shrewd reply. "Do you know anything about vampires and their ways?"

She was determined to bluff the situation out. "Why should I?"

"No reason except that you're thinking about marrying Barnabas and he may be one," the youth warned her. "Vampires are walking dead who live in coffins during the day and stalk the night world. And they have to have human blood to survive. So they attack people and drain blood from them. Every now and then they take too much blood and someone dies. Or maybe they attack to avenge and kill the same way. Vampires make dangerous enemies!"

"You seem to be very well informed."

"In Collinsport it pays to be," the youth said grimly. "Two years ago we had a lot of cases of young women being found wandering in the night with their minds a blank and a red mark on their throats. When they came to they all had stories about some black phantom attacking them."

She smiled scornfully. "It sounds like village girls indulging in a group hysteria or giving out a wild story to attract attention to themselves."

"It was more than that," he said determinedly. "What about the marks on their throats?"

"They could have made them themselves."

Jim Collins smiled scornfully. "You are on Barnabas' side, aren't you? If you want to help him you'd do well to tell him a lot of folk are watching him. And if there are any new ghostly goings-on he's liable to find himself in a heap of trouble."

"Why don't you tell him?" she asked defiantly.

Jim looked wise. "I guess he'd take it better from you."

"You're saying you are afraid of Barnabas?"

Jim shook his head. "No, but I don't find him easy to talk to. Neither does my father."

"When Dr. Padrel cures your Uncle Barnabas of his illness you'll all feel ashamed," she warned him. "And I hope then you'll ask him to forgive you for the wild things you've believed about him."

"My father says Dr. Padrel is a charlatan," Jim told her.

"How can he possibly know that?"

"My father is a pretty good judge of people and so am I," the youth assured her. "And I don't like that Padrel either, though he has a pretty daughter."

Diana smiled thinly. "Pretty girls seem to interest you."

"Only special ones. You do."

"Thank you," she said primly. "We should be starting back. I'm to meet Barnabas by the old house."

She turned and walked back along the path, and Jim kept in step with her. "It's getting near dusk. He'll show himself soon," he said.

"I don't think the exact moment of dusk has anything to do with it," she said, looking straight ahead and avoiding his eyes.

"Maybe you're wrong about that," he remarked mockingly. "Vampires always emerge at dusk."

"You're the only one who thinks Barnabas is a vampire."

"Wrong again," he said. "But I tell you what I do think. I think you're pretty and wonderful and it would be a crime for you to marry anyone like Barnabas."

She walked more swiftly in an effort to get away from him. "I don't want to hear any more such talk."

"All right, I won't say anything," he promised. "But I like you and I'm only trying to help you."

"Thanks," she said with a hint of sarcasm and diverged from him to take a linking path that led from the cliffs to the outbuildings and the old house beyond where Barnabas was staying. Her cheeks were burning with anger and embarrassment. The dreadful part of it was that the likable Jim Collins was so close to the truth. In spite of her resentment of his frankness, she knew that it was best he'd talked to her as he had. She could at least warn Barnabas.

The gray tint of dusk was cloaking the estate as she neared the old house. She was wearing a muslin dress and had a silk scarf around her shoulders as protection against the evening cold. It was cool here in Maine. She thought of the hot days and nights in Italy as a nightmare ended. Ahead she saw the tall, courtly figure of Barnabas appear on the steps. Then he came towards her.

He was smiling as he came up to her and took her in his arms. His cold lips touched hers and then he surveyed her at arm's length. "You look strangely upset," he said. "What is wrong?"

"I am upset," she agreed. "I've just been talking to Jim."

He looked resigned. "I fear my relative is not one of my admirers."

"He spoke of a number of things I'm sure you should know."

"Such as?"

She told him quickly, skipping the details to give him the main facts. He listened with a growing look of cynicism on his face.

"I realize I am a good deal less than welcome here," he admitted. "But it seemed the ideal place for Dr. Padrel to treat me."

"You must be careful," she cautioned him. "The people in the village are already suspicious of you. If anything happens while you are here they are bound to blame you."

Barnabas nodded grimly. "That superstitious lot have always been too quick to make me a scapegoat."

Her pretty face was dark with worry. "I know the terrible risk you take all the while you remain here. In the daytime you are completely defenseless. If they should find you in your coffin they could kill you while you slept. Peters wouldn't be able to stave off a crowd."

"I have no choice but to take the risk."

"Why couldn't you move down to the other house?" she wanted to know. "Then Dr. Padrel could protect you. It seems to me you'd do better to remain there all the time. He'd be more apt to hurry with preparing your treatments."

"I won't stay there," Barnabas said sharply. "I have always remained at the old house during my visits back. I won't change my pattern to please a few ignorant louts."

"Ignorant louts cause most of the trouble in this world," she reminded him bitterly.

The handsome Barnabas smiled at her. "Now you're indulging in some philosophy. I think we shouldn't be wasting our time in such an idle fashion. We'd better stroll over to Dr. Padrel's and see if he's ready to begin my treatments yet."

"I agree," she said.

"I have an idea Jim has more than a casual interest in you," Barnabas said. "I noticed his eyes never left you after you met last night."

She blushed. "He's only a boy."

"Man enough to be looking for a wife," Barnabas corrected her. "And human enough to be jealous of any man who has won a handsome young woman like you."

"I have tried not to give him any encouragement," she said worriedly.

Barnabas chuckled and took her by the arm. "Young men of his age and temperament scarcely require any encouragement," he said as he led her along the path. It was almost completely dark by the time they arrived at the great white mansion where Dr. Padrel and Maria were living. When they got there they were surprised to see a horse and buggy waiting outside the front entrance. As they reached the door it opened to reveal the odd Dr. Padrel about to show a pleasant, dark-haired young man out.

"You have arrived at an opportune moment," Dr. Padrel said at once. "This is Dr. Robert Stuben from the village. He has been here seeing Maria. She took a bad turn this afternoon. I fear the trip was too much for her."

"That's very unfortunate," Barnabas said quietly. And addressing the young doctor, he added, "I believe I did meet you when I was visiting here two years ago. One evening we enjoyed a drink at the bar in the Blue Whale."

The young doctor stared at Barnabas. "Of course, now I remember. You are a cousin of Stephen Collins."

"Exactly," Barnabas said. "And this is my friend, Miss Diana Hastings."

"I'm happy to meet you. Miss Hastings," the young man in brown tweeds said politely. "It's too bad your visit here is to be marred by the illness of Miss Padrel."

"Is she very ill?" Diana asked.

"She appears weak and has a fever," the young doctor said. "I shall come back tomorrow and will be better able to make a diagnosis then."

"Thank you," Dr. Padrel said. "I will depend on your returning."

Dr. Stuben climbed up into the buggy and, with a final nod to them, drove off. Then Diana and Barnabas entered the lamplit hallway of the white house. Diana saw that Dr. Padrel was in a troubled state.

He shook his head as he closed the door after them. "I tell

you I am baffled by this sudden change in Maria."

Diana asked, "May we see her for a moment?"

The doctor looked gloomy. "That would not be practical," he said. "Dr. Stuben has given her a sedative. It is important that she get some rest."

Barnabas stood there frowning. "Didn't you feel equal to treating her without calling in another doctor?"

Dr. Padrel's eyes blinked rapidly. "A father rarely likes to take full responsibility for a sick son or daughter. I decided a consultation was in order."

"And thus far Dr. Stuben hasn't been able to help," Diana said.

"Unfortunately, no," he said, staring grimly at the floor. "I have long known that Maria would die before many months passed. Now that I am confronted with the reality, I realize that I haven't truly accepted it."

Diana felt a surge of sympathy for the odd old man. "That is quite understandable."

"She seemed well enough when we got off the night boat," Barnabas said in a strained voice. "Have you any idea when this latest setback in her health began?"

Dr. Padrel raised his eyes to gaze at Barnabas sadly. "May I be frank?"

Barnabas shrugged. "Of course. As frank as you like."

The man with the big head gave her a hesitant glance. "You must forgive a distressed father, Miss Hastings. But I feel the time has come for me to speak my mind."

She began to feel uneasy. She had an idea he was up to some wily trick. She still couldn't have confidence in the strange old man. "Please speak freely," she said.

"Maria, like her late mother, is a creature of delicate heart. A most impressionable girl." He turned to Barnabas. "You will remember during my last attempt to restore you to normalcy she was around a great deal. She was delighted to act as your nurse."

"For which I shall forever be grateful," Barnabas said.

Dr. Padrel rubbed his hands together nervously, the thin knuckles glistening in the soft lamplight. "I believe it was at that time my daughter fell in love with you," he said.

Barnabas seemed astonished. "But I gave her no reason to think I had any tender sentiments for her."

Dr. Padrel sighed. "I believe that. But my daughter is not a worldly girl and I think she mistook your friendship for a sign of deep affection."

"I'm sorry," Barnabas said. "I truly am."

"It was not your fault," the girl's father went on in his cunning way. "And the crisis did not come until Miss Hastings appeared on the scene. Then my daughter became aware of your feelings for Miss Hastings. I must say this hit her hard. And it was from then on that she began to wilt."

Diana felt she could remain silent no longer. Addressing herself to the doctor, she said, "I'm sorry I've brought your daughter unhappiness. But from all that Barnabas has said, it seems clear that he gave Maria no encouragement."

"True," the doctor said sadly. "My daughter allowed her dreams of a possible romance to wholly control her. And I was guilty of the same thing. Knowing Maria would not live long, I began to hope that you might, out of pity, make her your wife for the last few months of her life."

Barnabas looked astounded. "But that would be a very wrong thing to do. I'd have no right marrying Maria unless I loved her."

"That is so," Dr. Padrel said, his eyes showing blank despair.

"Surely with the help of Dr. Stuben your daughter will improve," Diana said.

Dr. Padrel looked doubtful. "How can one mend a broken heart?" he asked.

"I'm certain that when I'm able to speak with her I'll clear up all this misunderstanding," Barnabas contended.

"Perhaps," Dr. Padrel said, but he sounded doubtful as they all stood there hesitantly in the hallway of the big white house.

Barnabas said, "Our actual reason for coming here was to see how you were making out installing your laboratory. I'm anxious to have the experiments begin."

Dr. Padrel revealed a stubborn expression. "I have been too upset by Maria's illness to manage much work on the project."

"That's disappointing!" Barnabas said sharply. "I have spent a lot of money and effort to bring you here."

"Granted. But I must have peace of mind in which to work."

Diana stared at him. "Haven't you done anything at all?" She was alarmed for Barnabas. It was vital that the experiments get underway and he be helped.

The doctor looked nervous. "I have installed some of the equipment," he said.

"May we see what you have done?" Diana wanted to know.

Dr. Padrel looked as if he was about to refuse this privilege when Barnabas said, "Yes. I think that would be wise."

He gave way before their firm requests. "Very well," he said. "Please follow me."

He lit a candle and, holding it aloft, led them down a narrow dark hallway to the rear of the house which overlooked the ocean. There he opened a door and led them into a big room with several tables on which were set up a forest of test tubes and other scientific paraphernalia.

The glow of the candle bathed the equipment in a soft light but left the balance of the big room shadowed. Dr. Padrel's head and shoulders were also mantled by the candle's glow. Diana was again struck by his odd appearance, and it seemed to her there was an air of deceit about him which he could not conceal.

Regarding the crowded tables of equipment, Diana said, "All this is very imposing, but when do you begin treating Barnabas?"

The man holding the candle eyed her coldly from behind the square spectacles. "That is hard to say. It depends on Maria's condition."

"I beg you to hurry," Barnabas said.

The doctor nodded. "I understand. But you will agree it is hard to see a daughter pine and waste away."

"You have my sympathy," Barnabas said, with sincere emotion in his tone.

"And mine," Diana said. "But things are uneasy in the village. I think you should find out as soon as possible whether you can aid Barnabas with your new treatment."

"I'm more anxious to discover that than anyone," Dr. Padrel insisted, but there was little conviction in his manner. "It will be considered a miracle if I can make Mr. Collins a normal man again. And I desire more than anything to have my work recognized. Yet there is one other miracle that would be even more satisfying than the dispelling of the vampire curse."

"What would that be?" Barnabas asked.

The candle flickered giving a strange expression to the alchemist's face. "I would like to be able to give Maria a new body," he said. "A strong healthy body to see her through years of life. If I could but transfer her head with all its beauty and brains to a strong body I would consider my poor talents had been used to the fullest advantage."

The macabre suggestion brought a cold fear to Diana. "Would such a transfer be desirable even if it were possible? Would the personality survive? What a shocking thing to end up with Maria having a healthy body and a disordered mind! I think madness would be the price of such success."

The eyes behind the glasses met hers balefully. "I do not agree," the doctor said. "And I shall not give up hope that such a transplant will one day be successful. Indeed I predict it will be commonplace to substitute many vital organs such as the kidney, lung or even the heart. The healthy members will be removed from the newly dead and used to replace diseased organs in those still alive but dying."

Barnabas nodded. "It should not be impossible. But forgive

me if I must concentrate first on my own problem. Will you attempt to get things in order so you may give me the first treatment tomorrow night?"

"I will make every attempt to do so," he said, leading them out of his newly established laboratory.

At the front entrance of the house both Barnabas and Diana expressed their wish to come and visit Maria when she was feeling better. The doctor vaguely thanked them and promised he would let them know when this was possible. But again Diana was troubled by the lack of sincerity in his manner.

As she and Barnabas walked away from the big white mansion she drew her shawl around her and shivered. "It is suddenly cold," she said.

"Maine nights are often like this," he agreed.

She glanced up at him. "What do you make of the way Dr. Padrel is proceeding?"

"It's not very satisfactory," Barnabas said in a tight voice. "Especially as the situation in Collinsport is hostile."

"I was shocked by that story of Maria being in love with you."

"I had no idea she had any serious interest in me," Barnabas agreed.

"And the brazen way in which her father brought it out," Diana went on. "I believe he's still trying to get you to marry the girl. He thinks his story that she has only a few months to live might make you more willing. It could be a trick. The girl might not really be all that ill."

They were walking along the cliff path and Barnabas suddenly halted and stared at her. "They wouldn't dare try anything like that!"

"Why not?"

His face showed concern. "What could be their motive? Would any man want his daughter to marry a vampire? Dr. Padrel knows my secret."

"He also knows you are tremendously wealthy and that he would have a strong hold over you. His whole story of being able to cure you could be a bluff."

"I don't want to think that!"

"Nor do I," she said at once. "But we must try to see this clearly, Barnabas. He has full knowledge of what you are and he can use it against you if he likes."

"I'm paying him well to cure me."

"If he ever had any intention of doing that, or is even capable of doing it, I think he's lost his interest," she argued. "Now he is considering the transference of Maria's head to somebody's healthy body."

"It's too fantastic," Barnabas protested.

She studied his gaunt face in the moonlight. "No more fantastic than your own predicament. I think if Maria really has consumption he is going to attempt some such weird experiment. I think it has his full attention now and he will go ahead with it before he tries to help you."

Barnabas frowned. "If I were sure of that I'd find a way to stop him."

Diana's eyes met his. "There is one other thing."

"Yes?"

"I know that you have been taking blood from Maria. I saw you do it that night on the ship. I don't question your need for it. But I do wonder if your actions haven't helped weaken her."

The handsome features of the man in the caped-coat showed emotion. "I'm troubled that you saw what you did. I was very ill that night. I had to have blood."

"You haven't answered my question," Diana said quietly. "Did you harm Maria?"

"No. Dr. Padrel was aware of my needs and what I had to do. He gave me his full approval on the condition I withdrew only a minimum amount of blood. And that is what I did."

"What a horrible thing for you to have to cope with," she said in weary dismay. "How is it all going to end, Barnabas?"

He took her by the arms. "Dr. Padrel is going to cure me. We must believe that. I know he can do it if he wishes."

She stared up into his face, and tormented by the stricken look she saw there, she said in a frightened whisper, "Yes. We must believe that."

Barnabas continued to grasp her arms for a long moment after she finished speaking. She sensed that he wanted to kiss her but could not bring himself to touch those cold lips that had so often preyed on others for blood to hers in a gesture of love. The barrier of his vampire lusts had suddenly intruded between them.

He let her go. "I'm sorry, Diana," he said in a hushed voice and turned from her to stare out across the moonlit water.

She touched her hand to his arm. "I don't hate you for what you are, Barnabas," she said. "It's just that it's hard to understand at times."

Still looking away, he said, "It was a mistake to bring you here. I should have seen you safely back to London and waited until I was certain Dr. Padrel could cure me."

"No," she protested. "I want to be with you in this ordeal. I want to help. And if you need my blood, that will be all right. Come to me rather than expose yourself to attack by preying on any of the village girls."

Barnabas wheeled on her with an angry look. "Do you think I

would do that?"

"I wouldn't mind. It would make me feel part of it."

"And when I was cured you would still remember the terror of my lips on your throat! Of my selfishly draining your blood for my own survival! I do not want my wife to have such memories of me!"

She was startled by the intensity of his reply. "I'm sorry, Barnabas. I only wanted to help."

"You can help best by closing your eyes to the things I do not want you to see," he said bitterly. "Come! It is time I took you back to Collinwood."

They hardly spoke at all during the rest of the walk back, and the goodnight between them was brief with no kiss exchanged. She could tell that Barnabas was still rankling from her revelation that she had seen him in the role of a vampire. She quietly made her way upstairs to her room. The big house was silent except for the wash of the waves on the nearby beach.

She fell asleep as soon as she was in bed, but then she was caught up in a nightmare which made her thrash about and moan pitifully. She was back in Italy. The heat was worse than ever. She was crouching in a shadowed room and barely able to breathe. Her wrists were shackled to her ankles with a heavy set of chains. Every time she tried to move it hurt. Next, the door to the room opened and the dark-suited estate manager came in.

He walked over to her and, bending down so that his face was close to hers, told her that the mad Count of Baraga was on his way to marry her. She cried out in protest but the Satanic-looking estate manager merely laughed at her. And when she tried to escape from the room he hurled her back on the stone floor and the metal bands cut into her wrists and ankles.

She was stretched out there sobbing when she heard footsteps and when she looked up she saw the Count entering the room with Dr. Padrel at his side. The doctor was dressed in the robes of a priest and the Count wore a simpering smile on his reptilian face.

Coming close to her he giggled and said, "The doctor is going to marry us!"

She shook her head. "No!"

The Count merely giggled again and then Dr. Padrel took his place before them and began to intone a lot of gibberish. The estate manager stood by and smiled evilly as the ceremony proceeded. Diana screamed again and again that she would not become the Count's wife, but the doctor kept on droning out a bedlam of words.

She woke up screaming! Then she quickly realized it had all been a dream. Sinking back on her pillow she discovered that her temples were damp with perspiration. Feeling guilty, she hoped that she had not disturbed the others with her wild nightmare. Though it remained vivid to her as she stared up into the darkness, she knew how fantastic it had been.

The mad Count of Baraga could threaten her no more. She had seen Barnabas crush him with one of his horrible statues. And the estate manager had fallen to his death from a high window of the castle. As for Dr. Padrel, he had never known the other two. She had merely mingled them together in her imagination because she'd hated and mistrusted all three of them.

Yet she had only the rather sinister Dr. Padrel to deal with here. She could not share the optimism of Barnabas in feeling the alchemist was going to cure him, but she did not know what to do about it. Young Jim Collins had pointed out that neither he nor his father had any confidence in Dr. Padrel. They had dubbed him a charlatan.

In her opinion he was that at least. He could even be a kind of criminal. It seemed to her he was attempting to use his daughter and her illness to trap Barnabas. Feeling he had failed in that, it appeared he was up to some other contemptible scheme.

When she went downstairs the following morning she was apprehensive that some of the others must have heard her screaming in her nightmare and would ask her about it. But none of them did. She was feeling somewhat relaxed when Jim Collins took her aside in the hallway.

"I have some news for you before I leave for the wharf," he said, a solemn look on his bronzed young face. "Last night one of our maids was attacked. She's still in her room weak and confused. She doesn't know what happened to her. But there are strange red marks on her throat." He paused significantly. "I don't suppose that could have anything to do with Cousin Barnabas!"

CHAPTER 7

Diana met the young man's stern glance. "Aren't you being rather unfair?" she asked. It was a part she had to play whether she liked it or not. She had to protect Barnabas.

"I don't think so," Jim Collins said quietly. "Nothing like that has happened in Collinsport since Barnabas left two years ago."

"I'm sure it has to be coincidence," she insisted.

He smiled wryly. "You'll have a hard time convincing the village people of that."

"If the girl wasn't badly hurt, I don't see why you are making so much of it," she said.

"The next one attacked might be killed."

"I'm sure you're being much too hysterical about the whole business," she said. "Because Barnabas is an individualist who likes to dress and behave differently from the average person, all the local people regard him with undue suspicion. And that includes you!"

The young man offered her another of his bitter smiles. "Sorry you see me in that light. I was hoping you'd come to like me."

"I would if you'd allow it," she said. "But I don't care for displays of narrow-mindedness."

"No one has ever accused me of being narrow-minded before."

"Perhaps you've never deserved it before."

He stared at her with some concern. "You're really in love with Barnabas, aren't you? You can't see any evil in him at all. You prefer to shut your eyes to the truth."

"My feelings for Barnabas are my private concern," she said, the blood mounting to her cheeks. "But I know him to be a gentleman. And a brave one. He saved my life in Italy."

"I hope you come to your senses," Jim replied disconcertingly, and with a significant parting look he opened the door and went out.

She stood there thinking about what he'd said. She had no doubts that it was Barnabas who'd attacked the servant girl. Before she'd left him last night she'd warned him against such activities and offered him her own blood. But he'd turned down her offer. She could only pray that the doctor would live up to his promises and cure Barnabas before events got completely out of hand.

As she turned to go up the stairs she was surprised to discover a painting of Barnabas on the wall. He had not mentioned it to her and in the short time of her stay at Collinwood it had not come to her attention. Now she studied the portrait and marveled that it was so accurate. In the long years of his exile as a vampire the handsome Barnabas had changed little. His strength of character showed in the gaunt, melancholy face.

"Admiring Barnabas?" It was Maude Collins who put the question to her. She had come silently up beside her.

Diana turned to her with a faint smile. "It is a fine portrait."

"1 think so," the older woman agreed, staring at it. "But Stephen wanted me to take it down and store it in the cellar."

"Oh?"

Maude Collins looked resigned. "When my husband gets a notion, it is hard to change his mind. There has been a lot of idle talk about Cousin Barnabas and I guess it upset him."

Diana pretended astonishment. "What sort of idle talk?"

Looking embarrassed, the other woman said, "It's not the sort of thing I should repeat to you who plan to marry him."

"Perhaps I should hear it," she suggested. She felt she should learn how the various members of the household felt so she could warn Barnabas. None of them guessed she was a party to his dreadful secret. Indeed, none of them knew his sad history so well.

Maude Collins' pleasant face wrinkled in an anxious manner. "Some strange tales have been spread about Cousin Barnabas. A lot of them started from the way he rests all day without seeing anyone and wanders about at night."

"In the cities many people do that."

"I try to tell Stephen that," his wife complained, "but he refuses to listen. I do believe he's like the rest of the ignorant villagers. Afraid that Barnabas is some kind of graveyard ghoul!"

"Graveyard ghoul?"

"People say they've seen him wandering about the family cemetery in the night when it's been raining, though how they would know unless they were there themselves is beyond me. And if they were there, it couldn't have been for any good reason."

"It sounds like a fabricated story," Diana said.

"That's what I think," Maude Collins agreed. "But the stories don't stop at that. They tell that Barnabas is a kind of phantom himself. A vampire like his grandfather, who left here because of a scandal of that sort. They say he bites the throats of young girls and drains them of blood."

"It's unfair to blame him for things his grandfather was accused of," Diana protested. Secretly she wondered what the woman's reaction would be if she knew the truth. That the Barnabas Collins now living at the old house was the same one who had left in disgrace nearly a century before.

"I have always liked Barnabas," Maude declared, "though Stephen and the boys can't abide him. But I say he has a right to return here if he likes. He is a Collins."

"He must appreciate your fairness."

"It's something we don't discuss. But I'm worried that his present visit may mean more trouble for him than pleasure. And I'm sorry he brought you along. You may be exposed to some trouble."

Diana stared at her. "Do you really think it's that bad?"

"Yes. According to Jim, the men who were on the wharf when Barnabas got off the night boat talked about forcibly putting him on board it again. They also discussed tarring and feathering him and running him out of the village that way."

"Why should they hate him so?"

"Because they think when he was here two years ago he molested a number of young girls. To make matters worse, one of our kitchen girls had a strange experience last night which seems to fit in with it all."

"What sort of experience?"

"She was out with her young man, a lad from the next farm. When they parted she came around to the back door. As she was about to come in she says a phantom figure in black sprang at her from the shadows. She couldn't see his face but he held her tightly and sank his teeth into her throat."

"It's a fantastic story," Diana exclaimed. "She must be

making it up."

"I don't know," the older woman worried. "She does seem still in a kind of trance and there are red marks on her throat."

"The farm boy could be responsible for them," Diana was quick to say. "The rest could be pure fakery to cover her staying out later than she should."

Maude Collins raised her eyebrows. "How did you guess she was out later than we allow?"

"It was obvious. Bound to be part of it."

"Whether that's the truth of it or not, the incident is going to start a number of ugly stories against Barnabas once again. People will blame him for being the phantom."

"I hope it doesn't get around," Diana worried. "Especially as I guess the girl's story is probably a tissue of lies."

"You may well be right," the older woman sighed. "I've come from the girl now and she still is babbling two or three versions of her story. So she's bound to start hostility towards Barnabas again."

"I must warn him tonight."

"You can if you like. The best advice you can give him is to show himself more in the daylight."

"He may not want to do it."

"If the talk goes on he may have to do it," Maude contended. "Stephen was grumbling about taking the portrait down only this morning and I'd say that's the first time he's mentioned it lately."

"Try to change his opinion of Barnabas," Diana urged. "I can promise you your husband's cousin is a fine man."

"I hope so. For your sake." The woman's eyes fixed on her worriedly. "There's been so much said. I wouldn't want to see you married to him if there was anything badly wrong."

"Thank you," she said gratefully. "I'm not worried."

Maude Collins studied the portrait of Barnabas once more. "Until they prove something else against him he remains there on the wall."

"I admire your stand."

The other woman said, "It's the way I feel. I do hope you and Barnabas get married and are happy. It strikes me that a good wife could do a lot for him."

Diana managed a wan smile. "I'm of the same opinion."

"I wouldn't put the wedding off too long."

"I don't mean to."

"And for his own sake I'd try to talk Barnabas into leaving Collinsport until things quiet down."

"I'll do my best," she promised.

Maude Collins smiled. "It's a lovely morning. You should go out in the sun and enjoy it."

She followed Maude's instructions and strolled across the lawn in the warm sunshine. Her voluminous orange skirt billowed in the slight breeze as she walked. But her thoughts were far away. She was not really enjoying the lovely morning. Rather, she was attempting to see some way out of the problem facing Barnabas.

The warm sunshine made her all the more conscious of him back there in the old house. Peters said he had a special room prepared in the cellars for his coffin. Down in the darkness there Barnabas would be stretched out in his casket, hands folded upon his chest, his eyes closed and his skin returned to the cadaverous tint that sometimes came over it. To all intents he was a dead man.

And yet, with the coming of dusk, his spirit would stir and he would rise to life again. She would have his company in the few hours until the approach of dawn. It wasn't enough. The only hope was that he could rid himself of the curse. And Dr. Padrel was about to make his second attempt to cure him.

Was the doctor a miserable faker? That was what tormented her. In the conversation with him last night it seemed that he had made a fumbling and brazen attempt to get Barnabas to marry his ailing daughter, Maria. She was still afraid that this was the sole reason the wily doctor had claimed he had a miraculous cure for Barnabas. He had hoped all along to get him to marry Maria and so gain control of the wealth Barnabas had in plenty.

She was halted in her reverie by the sight of a horse and carriage approaching. She shaded her eyes against the sun and watched as it came nearer. In a few minutes she recognized it as the rig belonging to young Dr. Robert Stuben, and she recalled that he had promised to visit the stricken Maria again in the morning. Perhaps he was coming to Collinwood now with some word concerning her. With that thought she hurried across the lawn to greet the carriage.

"Good morning, Miss Hastings," he said with a faint smile. "Pleasant seeing you so soon again." Tying the reins, he lightly jumped down from the carriage to stand facing her with his hat in hand.

She decided he had a strong face. The previous night she'd only had a brief look at him. Now she saw that his features were even and pleasant; shrewd gray eyes studied her from under dark eyebrows and he had long dark sideburns. His brown suit matched his hat. There was the air of a countryman about him and it was borne out by his tanned face.

"I suppose you have been to visit Maria Padrel," she said.

"I have," he said, instantly becoming serious. "I'd like to

speak with Mr. Barnabas Collins if I may."

"I'm sorry," she said. "That's impossible."

"It is?" The young doctor looked puzzled, then his expression changed as he seemed to recall something. "I remember now. He's the strange fellow who never leaves the house or sees anyone during the day."

"That is true. He suffers from insomnia and sleeps in the day."

Dr. Stuben nodded wisely. "Yes. So I understand. I met him one night at the Blue Whale and found him interesting. Then someone told me he was rather odd."

She smiled wanly. "Knowing the attitude of the villagers I'd expect they must have told you a good deal more than that."

"Yes," he said. "As a matter of fact they did. Hinted he had cloven hoofs and communicated with the Devil. That sort of thing. Our people may seem a stolid lot, but I can vouch for their lively imaginations."

Diana found herself liking the young doctor and hoping she might find some understanding of the dreadful plight she and Barnabas were in.

"You're the first one I've met who has discussed this sensibly," she said.

He looked resigned. "I'm not pretending to approve of the way Barnabas Collins lives when he's visiting here. He should know better than to draw attention to himself. There are some ignorant and superstitious people in the village, and they are capable of ugly actions under the right conditions."

"That's what frightens me," she admitted.

"You should discuss that with Collins," the young doctor said. "He's not doing himself any good."

"They're accusing him of being a vampire and attacking girls and all kinds of wild things," she exclaimed.

"I've heard the stories," he said calmly, his eyes appraising her. She noted that he hadn't indicated whether he believed them or not.

"I can take any message for Barnabas," she said, "and see that he gets it later."

"That's probably the best way then," Dr. Stuben said. "I've just been over to talk to Dr. Padrel."

"How is his daughter?"

He paused significantly. "Dr. Padrel behaved in a very eccentric fashion. He seems to have suddenly withdrawn into himself. After calling me in to attend his daughter, he now refuses to allow me to see her."

She stared at him in surprise. "He wouldn't let you see

her?"

"No. He was downright rude about it as well."

"What could make him behave that way?"

"I can't imagine," the young doctor confessed. "He was a very long while answering the door. When he did come he seemed confused and upset. He told me his daughter no longer required my services and closed the door in my face."

Diana was astonished. "What can it mean?"

He shrugged. "I can only assume the girl is better."

"But he was so concerned about her last night. He seemed certain she was near death."

The serious face of the good-looking doctor registered his bewilderment. "That is another thing I can't understand," he said.

"Yes?" She waited for him to explain.

"When I examined the girl I found her somewhat frail physically, but I saw no definite signs of the consumption which her father claimed had made serious inroads into her health."

Diana was again taken by surprise. For all Maria's bubbling spirits, she had accepted her father's verdict that the girl was near death. She had only begun to be suspicious when he had attempted to coerce Barnabas into marrying the girl.

She said, "Is it possible for her to be dying of consumption without your being aware of some of the indications?"

He hesitated. "It's barely possible. I'm only human with a human's tendency to make mistakes, but in the brief examination I was allowed I saw none of the usual signs of that wasting disease."

"I see," she said quietly.

"That was one of my reasons for wanting to see her again," he went on. "When I returned to my lodgings last night I checked a number of medical journals so I would be better prepared to make an examination of the girl today."

Her eyes met his. "Could that be the reason he wouldn't allow you to see her?"

"You mean he feared I might expose some sort of hoax on his part? That the girl wasn't really ill?"

"I was thinking that."

He frowned. "But if that were the case why should he call me in at all?"

"There is that to be explained," she admitted.

"I put the whole business down to Dr. Padrel's personal eccentricity. And that is why I would like to talk with Barnabas Collins. Since he is the one who brought the doctor here, he must know all about him. What are his medical qualifications, for instance?"

Diana hesitated. "I have no idea. I think he is more a

scientist than a medical man."

"You're suggesting he may not be a doctor at all?"

"It's possible."

Dr. Stuben seemed concerned. "I'm afraid the man is quite mad. And if that is the case, he may be neglecting his daughter when she really is in dire need of care."

"I doubt it," she said, her pretty face clouded. "Though I can't say it isn't the case. I have many views concerning Dr. Padrel myself, not all of them admiring."

The shrewd eyes searched her face. "Why did Barnabas Collins bring this odd man here?"

Again she faltered before replying. "Dr. Padrel is a scientist and Barnabas has high hopes for an experiment he is undertaking while staying in Collinsport. I believe he is financing the work."

"It is all very puzzling," he said.

"I agree."

"You will give my message to Barnabas?"

"I'll tell him all you've told me," she said.

"When I find time I'll come back to check with you again. Since I've been involved I'm worried about that young woman. Have Barnabas talk to the doctor and see what he can discover. If you feel I'm needed in a hurry, you can reach me at my place in the village."

"Mrs. Collins will know where you are?"

"Yes." He put on his hat, and offering her a faint smile, he said, "I hope when we meet next time we'll be able to keep our talk on a more personal and pleasant level."

"I hope so," she said sincerely. "And thank you for the interest you're taking in this."

"I am bothered by it," he admitted. "But the solution is likely simple enough. His daughter has probably improved and he doesn't want to be bothered by me."

He stepped up into the carriage and took up the reins. With a parting wave and smile he drove back in the direction of the village. She slowly walked towards the house with her mind filled with confused thoughts. What did this latest development mean?

She hadn't dared to talk freely to the nice young doctor however much he'd appealed to her. There was Barnabas to be protected. And while she had an idea the shrewd Dr. Stuben suspected there was a deep mystery about Barnabas, she didn't know exactly how much he'd guessed, so she'd been forced to be extra discreet.

She was inclined to agree with the young doctor that Dr. Padrel was mildly insane. In fact, she would go further and add that he was liable to be a fraud as well. As to his strange behavior regarding Maria, it could mean that she was better or worse. In either event, he might react in this crazy manner.

Until she and Barnabas could visit the doctor again, there was no telling what was going on. She saw little to be gained in trying to see Maria on her own. She was certain Dr. Padrel would find some excuse for sending her away. It was another instance where she'd have to mark time until after sundown.

When she reached the entrance to Collinwood she found Jim Collins standing on the steps. She gave him a surprised look and said, "I thought you were going to the wharf."

His tanned face had a mocking look. "I've been there and back. I see you have another friend, Dr. Stuben."

She blushed at his impudence. "Have you been spying on me?"

"I suppose so."

"Then I'd thank you not to."

"He's not a much better catch than Barnabas," Jim went on derisively. "He's a solemn young doctor who hardly gets a moment away from looking after his patients."

"And what is wrong with that?"

"His wife would hardly ever see him at home. You should look for a husband who'd devote all his time to you. Someone like me."

Diana gasped. "Well, I must admit you're not lacking in nerve."

"Think it over," he said with a crooked smile and left her to go around the house to the back.

She watched him go with a resigned smile on her face. The Collins family were all individualists and this young Jim was no exception. Yet in spite of his brashness, or perhaps because of it, she couldn't help liking him.

The balance of the pleasant day passed slowly. In the late afternoon she became so uneasy that she made up her mind to walk over to the old house and see if Peters might be around. She set out on the path that led to the outbuildings and the first Collinwood. It was also the path to the cemetery which lay at the bottom of a rolling field some distance beyond the old house and on the edge of a tall forest of evergreens.

As she neared the old house she saw the diminutive figure of Peters walking towards the field a long distance ahead of her. She supposed he was taking a solitary stroll to the cemetery and decided to follow him. It took her almost fifteen minutes to catch up with the little man. By that time he was standing inside the iron railing of the Collins family cemetery.

Peters was surprised when she joined him. "I had no idea I

would see you in this lonely place," he said.

She smiled sadly as she took in the forest of tombstones studded with an occasional vault. "I thought it might be interesting."

The small, bald man nodded affably. "I often come here when I have a little time to pass. It is also a favorite spot with Mr. Barnabas."

"When he awakes this evening will you tell him I urgently wish to speak with him?"

"Indeed, I will, miss. Is there something wrong?"

"I'm not sure. It has to do with Maria, Dr. Padrel's daughter."

"I shall certainly inform the master."

Diana looked around her. "Do they still bury here or is it just a relic of the past?"

"Oh, no, the cemetery is still in use," Peters said hastily. "In fact, there was a burial here this morning. A very sad case. The daughter of one of the farmers on the Collins land. She met her death by drowning in the bay. A fine healthy girl cut off in her prime."

"That is sad," she said. "I didn't hear anything about it."

"It was a quiet funeral," Peters explained. "I'll show you the grave. It's over here."

She followed the little man through a maze of gravestones and neat green mounds until they came to a fresh grave covered with rich dark earth. "Were you here for the burial?" she asked.

"Yes. I was the only one attending aside from Mr. Stephen Collins and the immediate members of the girl's family," he said. Then his small face creased in a frown. "I must admit I'm in error again. It's strange, but there was one other person attending though he stood a distance from the grave side. Dr. Padrel was here."

It gave her a start. She stared at Peters. "Are you positive?"

"Oh, yes, Miss Hastings," he assured her. "I couldn't mistake the doctor. He has, if I may say so, an unusual appearance."

"That is true," she said absently as she tried to find a reason for the doctor deserting his daughter and work at the big white mansion to attend the burial of an obscure country girl whom he'd never met.

"Josette DuPres is buried in this cemetery," Peters went on. "And old Joshua and many others. If these gravestones could speak, they would tell many a strange tale."

"I'm certain of that," she said. "You won't forget to give Barnabas my message?"

"No, Miss Hastings."

"I think I'll go back to Collinwood," she said. "It will soon be time for dinner."

By sunset she was out of the house and on her way to meet Barnabas. Since her talk with Peters in the cemetery a dreadful suspicion had been forming in her mind. She could scarcely wait to see Barnabas to discuss it with him. Peters had delivered her message and Barnabas met her on the path near the big barn.

He stood there in his caped coat with his silver wolf's-head cane in hand, and there was a worried expression on his handsome face. "What is all this I hear about Maria?"

Diana shook her head. "Barnabas, I don't know how to say it. I think Maria is dead!"

"Dead? Why do you think that?"

She quickly told him of her conversation with Dr. Stuben, ending with, "Padrel wouldn't allow him to see Maria and slammed the door in his face."

"And Dr. Stuben said he seemed in a crazed mood before that?"

"Yes. From the moment Dr. Padrel answered the door he behaved and talked strangely." She paused. "I believe he was crazed with grief because Maria had died."

Barnabas frowned. "We mustn't jump to conclusions."

"There is something else."

"Yes?"

"Peters told me Dr. Padrel attended the burial of a young girl who was drowned in the bay. The funeral was held in the cemetery this morning."

Surprised, Barnabas asked, "Why should he go there?"

Diana's eyes met his and she spoke in a meaningful tone, "Don't you remember what he said to us last night? That he believed it would be possible to transfer the head of one person to another person's body. And he wished that he had a healthy body to use to try and save Maria when she finally perished of her wasting illness."

"He can't have been serious!"

"I think he was," Diana insisted. "Suppose Maria died during the night and in his crazed state this morning he heard about the burial of that healthy young girl who was drowned. Isn't it possible he would go to the graveside out of curiosity?"

Barnabas nodded slowly. "I only pray this madness hasn't taken hold of him. That Maria is still alive."

"So do I," she said tensely. "But suppose she is dead; there's no telling what may happen. He may decide to try to go ahead with his monstrous experiment."

"I can't believe it."

"I don't want to," she said. "But he did talk about it. His idea being to keep Maria's head alive with a mechanical blood supply until he is able to find a healthy, recently dead body on which to graft it. What he hasn't taken into consideration is the strain on her mental powers. She would certainly go mad."

Horror of the idea showed in the deep-set eyes of Barnabas. "Collinwood has had enough of the monstrous," he said. "We must see the doctor and try to find out what has gone on. If Maria is truly dead we will have to reason with him. He must be dissuaded from attempting such an experiment that would surely desecrate Maria's body and produce a demented zombie!"

CHAPTER 8

Diana nodded weakly. "I agree, we must talk to him at once. I have only been waiting for you. Another awful result of all this is that he can hardly be giving any attention to preparations for beginning your cure."

"My fate must be set aside for the moment," he said. "First we must find out what has happened to Maria."

They hurried along the path past Collinwood and headed directly for the white mansion on the cliffs which Barnabas had leased for the scientist. They were both taut with excitement and a general fear of what the visit could produce.

Dusk cloaked the entire countryside by the time they reached the mansion. Diana saw that only a solitary light showed from an upper window. The rest of the great house was in darkness. It gave her a strange feeling and she felt on the border of nausea. She was growing more certain each moment that Maria was dead and the doctor had broken under the shock.

Arriving at the door, Barnabas rapped on it loudly with his cane. They waited and were answered only by an eerie stillness broken at the end by the melancholy cry of a night bird. Barnabas gave her a warning glance and with a frown repeated his rapping on the door with his cane. Then he shouted, "Dr. Padrel, it is Barnabas! I must talk with you!"

It was likely the shout that brought results. After long minutes there was a fumbling at the door from inside and it was gingerly opened. Dr. Padrel's head showed in the breach between door and frame. He carried a candle in a holder and his odd face showed a hostile expression. "I am busy," he announced. "I cannot be interrupted."

"What way is this to act?" Barnabas demanded sharply.

The scientist did not open the door further, but said, "You do not understand. I am at a most difficult point in my experiment. I cannot see you for a few nights. I must finish what I'm doing first. I will let you know."

Barnabas stepped close to the partly opened door as if he might force it open. "What is it you must finish?"

The strange doctor's pale blue eyes had an utterly mad gleam as he stared at them from behind the square-framed glasses. Then rather lamely he said, "But you do know what I'm doing. I'm slowly developing the serum which you must have to begin your cure."

"I thought you already had a small stock of the liquid with which to begin," Barnabas said.

"You misunderstood," Dr. Padrel maintained. "You have to be patient and you will allow me to work in complete privacy."

Diana stepped forward. "What about Maria?"

"Maria?" The scientist's face was highlighted by the candle in his hand and showed a blank expression.

She said, "You wouldn't allow Dr. Stuben to see her today."

"She is better. I did not need him."

Barnabas took up the questioning again. "The doctor claims you behaved very rudely and gave him no satisfaction about Maria's condition?"

Dr. Padrel scowled. "The young man insisted on arguing. I was worried that something would go wrong with the process while I was away from the laboratory. I had no time to reason with him."

"You're sure that Maria is all right?" Barnabas was stern in his questioning.

"She is much better."

Diana said, "Then surely we can see her."

"No!" The doctor almost screamed his refusal.

Barnabas looked worried. "I find that unreasonable."

"I cannot help what you think," he said. "I must do all this in my own way. You will go!" And he slammed the door shut and they could hear him bolting it on the inside.

It was dark now. Barnabas came down from the steps and stared at her in dismay. "I don't like this at all," he said.

"We didn't even have a chance to question him about being at that funeral today," she said.

"He would only have denied it."

"I suppose so."

Barnabas sighed deeply. "I'm beginning to think you may be right. Maria may have died."

"I told you."

"We can't be sure, of course."

"If you could get into the house some way, it should be easy enough to find out," she suggested.

"I've thought of that," Barnabas said bitterly. "But you forget that Dr. Padrel is familiar with my ability to transform myself into a bat-like creature. He will be especially careful to see no windows or side doors are left open."

"I say he is mad."

"It seems likely that he is," Barnabas said. "And with his sanity goes the last hope of my cure."

Diana pressed close to him. "I refuse to believe that. If Dr. Padrel disappoints you we shall search until we find another scientist ready to take on your case."

"I searched widely before I found Padrel," he reminded her.

"And he could very well be a charlatan," she said. "You may be better rid of him."

"In the meantime, there is Maria to consider. Living or dead, she needs help and protection. If the girl has died, I do not want him trying any of his macabre experiments on her."

"That may be what he is engaged in now."

"I hope not," Barnabas said. "I need to think about this. I don't want to try to force my way into the house with the help of others. There is just a tiny chance that Dr. Padrel is telling us the truth. Maria may be better and he may be working on the chemical process to begin my cure. I daren't risk spoiling that."

"It's such a small hope!"

"But still a hope."

"So we can't do anything?"

"Not for the moment," Barnabas admitted. "I will give him the night or two he has asked for. Then, if he does not begin my treatments we'll have to get help and make our way into the house and find what Deviltry he has been up to."

"It may be too late to protect Maria by then," she said. "He would have had time to transform her into a monster."

"It's a chance that has to be taken," the handsome, dark man said unhappily.

"I think you're wrong, Barnabas," she argued. "The house should be raided at once. The man is so obviously mad."

"And I beg you to listen to me and do as I suggest," Barnabas said.

"Very well." She turned away from the door of the white mansion with reluctance.

They slowly strolled back towards Collinwood. Along the way Barnabas repeated all his arguments in favor of giving Dr. Padrel the time he'd asked for. She listened quietly and still remained unconvinced. At last they reached Collinwood's front entrance.

"I need to think about this by myself," Barnabas told her. "I suggest you should go inside."

"But I'm too upset to sleep," she protested.

"There are dangers out here you should not expose yourself to," he said quietly.

"You are in danger too, Barnabas," she said anxiously. "More danger than you know."

"I'm used to living that way."

"But I can't bear to think of anything happening to you when you may be so close to being cured," she said.

He touched her arm gently. "I promise to be careful."

"But you never are! And the villagers are suspicious of you. It won't take much to have them rioting against you. They're already whispering you're in league with the Devil!"

Barnabas laughed lightly. "Then I should say I have a very resourceful associate."

"It is nothing to laugh about. They're afraid of you and they hate you."

"All of which I'm aware."

"You aren't safe in the old house with only Peters to guard you," she said. "I've told you that before."

"Don't concern yourself with it," Barnabas said quietly. "Our big problem is Dr. Padrel and what has happened to Maria. Let us concentrate on that."

"You always have the last word," she told him unhappily.

His answer was to enfold her in his arms for a lasting kiss. She welcomed his embrace, since he'd refused to kiss her the previous night. It was good to have the barrier between them shattered. His cold lips were as sweet to her as the warm ones of a normal man. She knew what he was and yet she loved him.

The kiss might have continued had there not been a footstep behind them. Barnabas quickly released her and turned to see who it was. A stern Stephen Collins emerged from the shadows to confront them accusingly.

The gray-haired master of Collinwood addressed himself to Barnabas, saying, "I have reached the limit of my patience with you, Cousin Barnabas."

Barnabas showed surprise. "I do not understand, Cousin Stephen."

"Because you are a Collins and my cousin I have closed my eyes to a great deal," Stephen Collins said coldly. "I even welcomed you back this time, and I've been glad to offer this young lady the hospitality of our home."

"For which I'm grateful," Barnabas said.

"You have a strange way of showing gratitude," Stephen Collins said with a curled lip.

"Why do you say that?"

"Need I tell you?"

"Yes."

Stephen Collins hesitated and glanced at her. "I have respect for this fine young lady," he said. "I dislike discussing this before her."

Diana spoke up. "Please don't mind me. If you have anything against Barnabas, I would like to hear it."

Stephen Collins lifted his eyebrows a trifle. "Very well. If it is your wish." And he turned to Barnabas once more. "Nora, one of our maids, was attacked here on the grounds last night. I'm certain you were the attacker."

Barnabas paled. "How can you be?"

"The facts of the case matched others that happened before while you were my guest," his cousin said bitterly. "I don't know what diabolical thing impels you to prey on these innocents. I don't care to know. But I no longer can countenance your behavior."

"So?" Barnabas said.

"So I'm warning you that you are no longer welcome on the estate," his cousin said. "I ask you to leave as soon as you can."

"I cannot go at once," Barnabas said. "There are valid reasons why I must remain."

Stephen Collins stared at him for a silent moment. Then he said, "You can do as you wish. I have warned you. And I can promise you no protection if the people of the village decide to deal with you on their own terms."

"I'll take that risk," Barnabas said quietly.

"Then it is on your own head," Stephen Collins said grimly. With a nod to her he moved on past them up the steps and went inside.

After he'd closed the door she gave Barnabas a pleading glance. "You heard him. He's telling you exactly what I did only in a different way. You are in danger."

"Nothing is going to happen," he said soothingly. "It is time to say goodnight."

She took her leave from Barnabas with a feeling of utter depression. She didn't see how she could stay on at Collinwood knowing the way Stephen Collins felt. Unlike Barnabas, she couldn't brush off the gray-haired man's angry words, yet she knew she could not leave as long as Barnabas remained. She had to do her best to protect him.

In her bedroom she paced up and down, quite unable to think of sleep. The only bright spot in the whole dark picture was her new friendship with the pleasant Dr. Stuben. She felt she could depend on him, and there was a strong chance she would soon need to enlist his aid.

It grew later and still she didn't want to go to bed. She kept seeing the frail, attractive Maria and wondering if the girl were still alive. Certainly Dr. Padrel had behaved like a madman when they visited him earlier in the night. What dark thing was going on in the shadows of that old mansion?

Casually she strolled over to the window and pulled back the heavy drapes to stare out across the lawn. And there in the moonlight she saw a solitary figure walking by the house. It was Dr. Padrel. He was walking like a man in a trance, his broad, puffy face showing a blank expression. But what made her gasp was the shovel he carried over his shoulder and the folded burlap on his arm.

Fascinated by the strange and unexpected appearance of the weird scientist she watched him until he was out of sight. It took her only a moment to guess where he was headed. It had to be the cemetery! It all fitted in with the other things she knew. And it explained why he had gone to lurk in the background at the funeral early in the day.

Maria must have died! And now he was on his way to rob the grave of the drowned girl. A girl whose body had been as healthy as poor Maria's had been diseased. She pictured him alone in the graveyard spading up the soft, black earth until his shovel grated on the lid of the coffin. Then he would descend into the grave, pry back the lid and gently lift the white-faced and placid corpse from her bed of satin.

The mad scientist would place her on the grass and wrap her body in the burlap. Next he would torturously bear her dead weight all the long way back to the mansion, where his magic would have preserved the live head of his beloved Maria. Only a madman would conceive and attempt to carry out such a plan. Once in his laboratory he would begin the complicated task of removing the head from the body of the drowned girl and restoring mechanical blood circulation to give the body life.

Only then would he attempt to attach Maria's head to the body! She forced herself out of the strange state these thoughts had induced and made up her mind she had to intervene. She would catch up with the madman and try to convince him that his plan was hopeless, that even if he gave Maria a new body she would have lost her mind. He must be made to see that and allow his daughter the solace of a normal death.

With this decision reached she quietly left her room and went down the stairs and out into the cool night. Everything seemed oddly silent and menacing at this late hour. She wished that she had roused Jim Collins and enlisted his aid. She was sure he would have been willing to help her, since he'd openly declared her attraction for him, but the mad scientist might be easier to handle if she approached him alone. So she would have to brave the threat of the night.

She reached the barns and heard the rumble of movement from the stables as the horses stirred restlessly, aware of her out there. Her heart pounding, she forced herself to go on. She could see no sign of Dr. Padrel in the darkness ahead and guessed that she had given him a longer start than she'd realized.

Suddenly without warning strong hands gripped her and circled her throat. Her attacker had silently stalked her from the rear. She tried to scream but only managed a strangled, choking sound. Thoughts of Barnabas came to her mind. Surely he was somewhere on the estate. Wouldn't he know she was in danger and come to rescue her? She prayed so. But she was beyond coherent thoughts now as the hands crushed out her very life. Eerie lights before her eyes gave way to a velvet blackness.

"Diana!" A familiar voice was calling to her from what seemed to be a great distance.

She tried to answer and couldn't. She stared up with frightened eyes and saw the anxious face of Jim Collins. She tried to say his name. Her lips moved but still she couldn't manage it.

"At least you're alive," he exclaimed with relief as he raised her head a little.

Diana felt idiotic and ashamed. She had made such a fool of herself. And her throat burned as if flames were dancing around it. She made a supreme effort and in a husky voice unlike her own said, "Someone!"

"I know," he said. "Someone tried to throttle you. Do you know who it was?"

"No." The single word was an effort.

"I didn't expect you would," the young man said with disgust. "You girls are all alike. You take chances with your lives and don't see anything."

"Meant to call on you," she managed.

"But you didn't," he reproved her. "I wouldn't have known you were out here if I hadn't heard the front door open and shut. I guessed something was doing and I came down."

"Saw man with shovel on path," she said.

Jim eyed her derisively. "It's my guess you've been having yourself a nightmare. Who ever heard of anyone going around with shovels at this time of night? Do you think you're well enough to stand up?"

She nodded, and at the same time she realized it would be impossible to explain her reasons for being out there to the young man. He knew nothing of the background events leading up to the dreadful moment she'd just gone through. She had to keep the facts to herself until she could contact Barnabas or perhaps Dr. Stuben.

Thought of Barnabas gave her some hope. There was a chance that he might have seen Dr. Padrel pass the old house on his grisly errand. If so, Barnabas would surely intercept him and prevent him despoiling the drowned girl's grave. The more she thought about it the more likely it seemed that this could happen.

But who had tried to strangle her and why? She could only think of the mad scientist as her attacker. He might have noticed her following him and been crafty enough to slink into the shadows to one side and wait until she came unsuspectingly by. Then he had leaped on her and choked her until he was satisfied she was dead. He'd almost managed it.

Jim assisted her to her feet and then supported her as she wavered. "Think you can make it back to the house?"

"In a minute."

The young man stood there as she gradually recovered. Staring grimly into the darkness around them, he said, "I think I know who it could have been."

She felt a pang of fear. "It could have been anyone," she murmured. And she knew this wouldn't satisfy him.

Jim gave her a significant look. "I warned you against Barnabas."

"It wasn't him!"

"You said you didn't see your attacker," he reminded her. "You'd better make up your mind."

She was anxious to get him off the subject. Weakly she told him, "I'm well enough to go back inside now."

He kept an arm around her waist to support her. She was still dizzy and walked unevenly. The pain at her throat was not so intense but it kept throbbing. The thing that troubled her most was that Barnabas might be blamed. And she daren't try to explain the real situation. No one would believe her if she did.

After what seemed an interminable journey they reached Collinwood and he assisted her up the front stairs and inside. When he'd safely deposited her on a divan near the living room door he said, "I'm going to call my father."

Diana sat up with alarm. "No. Please don't wake him. There's no need."

Jim frowned. "You were nearly murdered. He should know."

"The morning will be time enough. Let me go to my room. Rest is all I need."

"I should send a message to the village and have Dr. Stuben come out."

"That can wait also," she insisted. "If I think I need a doctor in the morning you can send for him. I'm feeling much better already. It was mostly shock and fear."

"You're trying to make little of it to protect Barnabas," the young man said standing above her accusingly.

"No!"

"It's plain enough," Jim replied bitterly. "But it's also plain to me that Barnabas did attack you. How can you be in love with a madman?"

"It couldn't have been him," she protested. "Barnabas would never do anything like that."

"He attacked one of our maids last night. My father has asked him to vacate the old house as soon as possible. We all believe Barnabas is a mental case or worse. Why do you blind yourself to his faults?"

Diana looked up at him with pleading eyes. "Please trust me. I think I know Barnabas and his problems better than any of you. Don't be so quick to condemn him. You're not being fair."

Jim hesitated. "Are you asking me to remain quiet about tonight? To deliberately protect him?"

"It would be generous on your part."

"You think I should wait until there is another victim?" The young man's tone was harsh.

"There shouldn't be any other victims," she said, rising though she still had a reeling head.

He studied her in silence for a long moment. "I won't wake up my father," he said at last. "But I make no other promises. It all depends on how you are in the morning."

She gave him a grateful smile. "Thank you," she said gently.

Jim shrugged. "I'll see you up to your room."

At her door she turned to him and said, "You're really a very nice boy."

"I'm a man!" he protested. "And I'm in love with you." And to prove both statements he took her in his arms without warning and kissed her. He let her go almost at once with a wry smile, saying, "I hope that may help to make you forget about Barnabas." He turned and went down the hall.

Diana hastily entered her room with the moist warmth of his kiss still on her lips. It was a startling climax to a wholly shattering series of events. She knew the young man admired her, but she'd not been prepared for this bold expression of his feelings. Things at

Collinwood were growing more complicated each day.

Somehow she managed to sleep. She awoke in the morning with a stiff throat and still showing signs of the violent attack that had been made on her. But she was feeling much better than she'd anticipated. It was raining outside and the gray day gave her a feeling of depression.

Forcing herself to get up, she quickly dressed. She wanted to speak to Jim before he left for work at the family fish-packing plant and assure him she wouldn't need a doctor after all. By the time she arrived downstairs he'd already finished breakfast and was in the hallway, apparently on his way out.

She called to him from the stairs. "Jim!"

The blond young man turned and seemed pleasantly surprised to see her. "I've been worrying about you," he said. "You look much better."

Diana went down the remaining stairs. "I'm all right. Please forget about last night."

His face shadowed. "I can't do that."

"Have you told your father?"

"I mentioned that you stumbled in the darkness and had a bad scare."

"That was all?"

"Yes. Though I did suggest it might be wise to send word to Dr. Stuben to come by and see you this morning. Just to be on the safe side."

"There was no need."

"It can't do any harm," he said. And with a meaningful look, he added, "After last night I hope you realize there are other men who love you besides Barnabas."

Diana blushed. "We were upset last night and not entirely responsible for our actions."

"I was," Jim said bluntly. "Remember that."

"You know so little of the truth of what is going on here," she warned him. "If you understood everything it would be different."

"I understand that Barnabas is a menace. That's enough."

"There are others perhaps more dangerous," she hinted.

"Who? He's the only one I know who prowls about in the darkness preying on young girls."

"The attack on your maid, Nora, as well as the one on me could have been made by some vicious stranger passing through the town. Some of the tramps who move from village to village have criminal records."

He looked grim. "I might be willing to listen to that and maybe believe it if this wasn't a repetition of things that had gone on here before, two years ago when Barnabas came to visit us."

"You've made up your mind."

"That's right," he said. "Be careful with the doctor when he comes. He's a charmer. But he'd make a rotten husband."

She smiled wanly. "I think you made a point of that before."

"No harm to remind you again," he said. "And don't go around risking that truly lovely throat of yours. This place isn't safe until we are rid of Barnabas."

Diana listened with mounting apprehension. All suspicion was pointing to Barnabas rather than to the malevolent Dr. Padrel. Everyone seemed blind to the strange scientist and the threat he was presenting to the village. She struggled to think of some way of hinting this which would seriously impress the young man standing facing her, but couldn't.

At that moment the front door opened and Stephen Collins entered. The austere gray-haired man was wearing a dark raincoat and hat and his lined face showed an expression more stern than usual.

Ignoring her, he addressed himself to Jim. "We'll have to delay going to the plant for a little. I want you to accompany me to the cemetery."

Jim's eyebrows raised. "To the cemetery?"

Revulsion showed on Stephen Collins' aristocratic features and in his tone as he said, "Yes. A most infamous incident has taken place. Some ghoul visited the cemetery last night and stole the body of that girl who drowned."

CHAPTER 9

Diana thought she might faint. Stephen Collins turned grimly to her and apparently at once noticed her shocked state. He immediately took on an apologetic air.

"I'm sorry to have mentioned this unhappy thing in your presence," he said.

"It is all right," she murmured.

Jim was all concern. He came to her and touched a hand to her arm. "You're in no shape for this kind of talk. Do you want to go back to your room?"

"Yes," she said. "I should."

"I'll take you there," Jim said, and he turned to his father. "I'll be back to go to the cemetery with you in a moment, Father."

"That will be fine," Stephen said. "And do let me offer my apologies again. Miss Hastings."

Jim was already helping her up the stairs. She closed her eyes and let him guide her. So Barnabas had not encountered Dr. Padrel and the old scientist had gone on to the cemetery and dug up the unfortunate girl's body. She dared not think beyond the facts of the case. What had the madman done with the body?

At her door Jim said, "I'll tell the housekeeper to have some strong tea sent up to you."

"Thank you," she said in a small voice.

"Dr. Stuben will soon be here. He can give you something to make you feel better. I must go."

"Yes."

His eyes met hers in a grave look. "Surely now you must be convinced that Barnabas is a menace. You can't continue to feel love for a man who would commit such a despicable act."

"Why blame Barnabas? He has no reason to rob graves!"

Jim frowned. "He has been seen lurking in the cemetery after dark. It seems to be an obsession with him. Who can explain the motives of a crazy man?"

"I don't believe Barnabas is insane."

"I doubt if you'll find many who think the same way," Jim warned her. "I must go and join my father."

Diana went into her room and walked over to the window to stare at the falling rain. As she looked out on the lawn she saw Jim and his father emerge from the front door in earnest conversation. Jim had put on a coat and cap against the rain and they both went around to the back of the house where they would undoubtedly be joined by some of the workers in the stable. The group would go to the private cemetery and make a careful examination of the area for clues as to who the graverobber or robbers might be.

In her mind was the vivid picture of Dr. Padrel with the shovel and burlap bag. He'd been walking in the direction of the cemetery when she'd first seen him. And she'd followed him a good distance of the way before she'd been attacked. No doubt he had been the one who'd struck at her. Then he'd gone on to complete his gruesome work.

For her part she had to believe that Maria was dead. What else would have made the madman behave so strangely towards everyone and then set out for the cemetery and steal the body? He hoped to perform a miraculous experiment and restore his beloved daughter to life. Diana believed the experiment was doomed to defeat. If so, what would Dr. Padrel's reaction be to failure? Would he brokenly admit his guilt and abstain from further insanity?

She fervently hoped so, for Barnabas' sake, since he was seemingly going to be the scapegoat for the alchemist's morbid depredations. Every mad act of Dr. Padrel's was going to be blamed on the man she loved. Somehow the doctor had to be stopped. From the beginning she had doubted his abilities. Now she felt Barnabas could expect nothing from him.

Time passed. A maid brought her up a tray of toast and tea. She sipped the hot black tea and tried to force herself to take some of the toast. Then there was a light knock on her door and she opened it to find Dr. Stuben standing there.

"May I come in?" he asked.

"Please do," she said. "I've been waiting for you." She closed the door after her. "Have you heard the latest?"

He put down his bag on a nearby table and stared at her in surprise. "If you mean your stumbling in the darkness last night, yes. Mr. Collins sent word about it this morning and asked me to come out and visit you."

She shook her head. "I didn't fall last night; I was attacked."

"Attacked?" His tone was sharp.

"And that's not what I was talking about. Something horrible happened here." And she went on to tell him about the girl's grave being robbed.

The young doctor heard her out and then asked, "It is your belief that Dr. Padrel did this?"

"I'm certain of it. I saw him walking towards the cemetery. He had a shovel and either burlap or canvas over his arm. It was when I followed him that someone tried to strangle me."

"A very strange story indeed," the young man said quietly.

She sensed an air of skepticism in him. "You do believe what I've told you?"

"I want to," he said. "But when the news of this grave robbery gets widely known in the village, it is Barnabas who will be blamed."

"I know," she said despairingly. "How can we shift the blame where it should be?"

"That is hard to say," he said. "Few people know of Dr. Padrel being here or would guess the kind of man he is."

"I think when his despair over Maria's death is complete he will collapse," she told him. "That moment will come when his macabre attempt to graft her head on the drowned girl's body fails. Then he may be willing to openly admit he was the one who robbed the grave."

He nodded. "That sounds reasonable."

"I'd like to go visit him now," she said eagerly. "It is possible he may talk to us."

Dr. Stuben was surprised. "I don't agree. I'd expect it might be just like yesterday. I doubt if we'd even gain entrance to the house."

"But shouldn't we try? If only to find out if Maria is still alive. And after last night's events, how can she be?"

"A good question," he said. "What about you?"

"My throat is stiff and sore. There's nothing that could be called serious injury."

His face shadowed. "I insist you let me examine you before we think of visiting Dr. Padrel. I won't have you going out in this bad weather until I know you are all right."

She sat meekly while he gave her injured throat a thorough check. When he'd finished he stood in front of her with a grim expression. "Now, I have a few pertinent questions to put to you."

Diana sensed that this could turn out to be a moment of crisis. She said, "Yes?"

"You came to Collinsport along with Barnabas, his servant and the Padrels. Up until now you've said little about yourself or your relationship with Barnabas, beyond the obvious fact you are romantically interested in him. I'd like to know how you met him and what led to your coming here in his company."

The way he had summed up the situation and the frankness of his approach came to her as a surprise. She said, "To answer all those questions will take a little time."

"I'm willing to spare it."

Diana sighed. "It began in London when I met Barnabas. I considered him the most charming man I'd ever known but my mother was opposed to our becoming engaged."

"So you ran off together?" the young doctor suggested.

"No. Nothing as simple as that, though I did seek out Barnabas and plead that we elope. He refused. But he promised that though my mother was taking me to Italy to visit the Count of Baraga, the son of one of my late father's friends, he would keep in close contact with me. In fact, he would follow me to Italy."

"And he did?"

"Fortunately, yes. The journey proved disastrous. My mother became ill and the Count and his estate manager had a villainous plot to force me to marry the Count. Since he was ugly and close to demented I rebelled. But my mother died and I was left in their clutches. It was then that Barnabas rescued me."

"And you came to America with him?"

"Not directly. We first traveled to an Italian seaport. While we were staying at an inn on the way Barnabas revealed the tragedy of his life and his reason for not eloping with me in London. He hoped that he soon would be in a position to marry me and asked me to come here with him. Dr. Padrel and Maria were joining us on shipboard as the doctor was going to treat Barnabas with a new serum he'd developed."

Dr. Stuben frowned. "I gather from all this that Barnabas is suffering from some obscure illness and this doctor has promised him a cure."

"Yes," Diana admitted. "I didn't like Dr. Padrel from the moment of our first meeting and I feared he might be merely trying to swindle Barnabas, but I had no idea he was tainted with madness then. Maria struck me as a pleasant young woman, innocent of her father's plotting and his attempts to get Barnabas to marry her."

"I didn't know about that."

"Yes. He's tried to persuade Barnabas to marry Maria, saying she has only a few months to live. Naturally, this upset me. But things did not get out of hand until we arrived here. Then Maria became very ill and Dr. Padrel did nothing to help Barnabas."

"We are at the place where Dr. Padrel refused to see me yesterday after enlisting my aid in doctoring Maria. I assume you and Barnabas went to visit him last night. Were you more successful in getting into the house?"

"Not at all. He wouldn't allow us in. And he showed no interest in starting the treatments that were supposed to cure Barnabas." She paused. "I think his story about having a serum is all part of his madness."

The young doctor studied her soberly. "Because of the many rumors here and because I know you to be a young woman of intelligence, I must ask one last and all important question."

She held her breath. "What is it?"

"Tell me the nature of the ailment from which Barnabas is suffering."

Now it was out in the open. The one person above all whom she trusted had thrown down the gauntlet. Was she going to take him into her confidence? Dared she risk telling him the truth about Barnabas? Could she expect him to go on helping them if she didn't?

After weighing it all carefully, she realized she had no choice. Giving the young physician an appealing glance, she said, "If I do confide in you, I must have your word you will not repeat any of what I say."

"You can depend on me."

"You may decide the true facts are even wilder than the rumors that have gone around the village."

"That is hardly likely," he said in a dry voice.

"Barnabas Collins is the original Barnabas who left here years ago under a cloud."

The young doctor looked at her incredulously. "What are you trying to have me believe?"

"That Barnabas Collins is a vampire, one of the living dead. He suffers under the curse of a girl called Angelique. And he has lived all down the years as a haunted wanderer."

"As a medical man I cannot admit the existence of vampires!"

"But they do exist," she maintained. "The living dead who rise up from their coffins in the dark hours and die again with the dawn. The ones thirsty for blood to renew their energies. The ones doomed to wander the earth forever unless someone drives a stake of hawthorn in their heart during their daytime sleep or they find one of the rare potions to cure them."

"And Dr. Padrel claims to have such a potion?"

"He tried before and failed. But this time he told Barnabas he was sure of success. He only needed a short time here to complete his experiments. You know how it has all turned out!"

The pleasant young doctor stared at her. "If I accept your version of things—that Barnabas is a vampire—how do you explain that you are able to love him?"

"Because he is a fine, noble man fighting against the curse. He may seek blood from his victims but he never harms them without just cause. I do love Barnabas and when he is cured I hope to marry him. I would marry him now but he refuses to consider it while he is still under the curse."

"And you're asking me to take his side? To defend him against the village?"

"I'm telling you that he needs a friend and deserves one," she said in a quiet voice.

He looked baffled. "How do you know that Barnabas is not as mad as this so-called doctor, and that all his nonsense about being a vampire is not a way to cover a murderous career?"

"I have implicit faith in him."

"I must confess I'm not so sure," the young doctor said worriedly. "But I will keep my word and consider all this in confidence. Did you intend to tell me your story or was it my questioning that decided you?"

"I knew I soon had to be honest with you. I feel you are my only friend here."

He smiled ruefully. "I want to be your friend. I can promise you that. But am I being sensible in considering furthering your romance with a vampire and trying to assist him?"

"Barnabas deserves your aid."

"We shall see," the doctor said with a sigh. "I am sure he will be in desperate danger when the grave robbery is voiced around."

"We should see Dr. Padrel at once and find out if there is any possibility of his confessing the crime."

"That sounds logical," he said. "But it is my idea that we will be met by a locked door. Are you ready to leave with me now?"

"As soon as I put on my cloak," she said. And she went to get it.

"Fortunately my rig has a cover against the rain," he said. "You shouldn't get too wet."

But when they went downstairs Maude Collins intercepted them and voiced her astonishment at Diana venturing out into the wet day. "After your accident last night, is it wise?" the older woman worried.

Dr. Stuben spoke up. "I'm calling on Miss Maria Padrel, who has been ill, and Diana is anxious to spend a little time with her."

This satisfied Maude and they left the house. The rain was still coming down heavily and they hurried across to the carriage. The young doctor saw her up on the seat and then took his place beside her. With a flick of the reins they were headed for the white mansion where Dr. Padrel was holding forth.

As the big mansion came into close view Diana began to feel uneasy. How would it go this time? She glanced at the profile of the good-looking Dr. Stuben and saw the thoughtful look he wore. She hoped he wasn't regretting his involvement in this frightening business. She ventured in a small voice, "We'll soon know."

"Yes," he agreed, without looking at her. "We'll soon know."

The young doctor rapped loudly on the heavy oak door. To Diana's amazement it opened almost at once, and Dr. Padrel stood there smiling at them.

"I'm glad you've come," he said. "I have been worried. Please step in out of the rain."

Dr. Stuben gave her a questioning glance as they took advantage of the strange scientist's offer. As soon as they were in the gloomy hall he shut the door to make the place even more shadowed.

The little man with the oversized head peered at them from behind the square spectacles, his pale blue eyes holding a frightened gleam. "I was so very stupid yesterday," he said. "And I was also insulting. Please forgive me. You caught me at a vital point in my preparation of the serum for Mr. Collins, and I could not bear being interrupted."

The young doctor frowned at him. "Are you giving this as a reason for turning us away and not allowing us to see your sick daughter?"

"Yes, though I think I explained that Maria has improved."

Diana spoke up. "But you wouldn't even see Barnabas last night. Why not, if you had the serum ready for him?"

The doctor's manner was apologetic. "Not quite ready, Miss Hastings. I was at the last important step. Tonight the serum is waiting for Barnabas to arrive. He shall have his first injection."

Diana didn't know what to make of it. The about-face on the part of Dr. Padrel was too much to accept. A glance at the young doctor told her he was just as astonished. The scientist was giving them such a fine reception, but it simply didn't ring true. There had to be something behind it!

And Diana began to feel she knew what it was. It was the madman's wily way of reacting to the failure of his experiment to give Maria life again. He had merely changed his tactics.

She said, "May we see Maria?"

"Of course," her father said promptly. "Though she does not need Dr. Stuben's attention any longer. I have given her a mild sedative and she is resting. But you may certainly look in on her for a moment."

They followed him down a narrow corridor and then he opened a door to a room overlooking the ocean. There, in a wide bed, was the frail Maria. Her eyes were closed but it was apparent she was sleeping rather than dead. After Dr. Padrel had given them long enough to have a good view of his daughter he closed the door again.

"Another day she will be well enough to talk to," he promised.

Diana left the room, at least satisfied that Maria was alive and on the way to recovery. But it didn't jibe in with the other things that had happened. Why had Dr. Padrel made that pilgrimage to the cemetery and stolen the drowned girl's body? Was he going to use it for some other hideous experiment?

Dr. Stuben must have felt the same way. When they got back to the gloomy hall he lingered to tell Dr. Padrel, "Miss Hastings believes she saw you going to the cemetery last night carrying a shovel. And this morning a body was found to have been stolen."

The broad puffy face took on a look of surprise. "You must be joking, Miss Hastings. I spent all day and most of the night over the test tubes in my laboratory."

"I'm certain it was you," she insisted. "I saw you from my window."

The pale blue eyes behind the square spectacles peered at her oddly. "You insist you could identify me at such a distance in the darkness?"

"It looked exactly like you," she said.

"But was it me?" Dr. Padrel asked with a triumphant pointing of his stubby finger at her. "I doubt if you would care to swear to it in a court of law or if they would accept your word."

Diana was becoming increasingly uneasy. "The man had a shovel on his shoulder and he was your size. He walked like you."

"Did you see the face clearly?" Dr. Padrel asked her. "Was it mine?"

"I couldn't make out the features clearly at that distance," she faltered. "But it looked like you. It had to be you. Who else would want to steal a body from the cemetery?"

Dr. Padrel looked from her to Dr. Stuben with a grim smile on his contrasting puffy face. "You see how illogical a young woman can be, Doctor? Though she was too far distant to identify this man, she claims it had to be me. That I was the only one who would be interested in stealing a body from its grave?" He wheeled around to face her angrily. "And why should I want to do that, Miss Hastings?"

"I don't know," she said weakly. "Perhaps to carry out some operation in trying to restore Maria to health."

"Maria is coming back to health," he snapped. "Your story is ridiculous, Miss Hastings. If you saw a man it was certainly not me."

"I'm sorry if I made an error," she said awkwardly.

"You should be," he replied sarcastically. "If I can be of no further assistance to you two young people, I should like to return to my work."

"Forgive the intrusion, Dr. Padrel," Dr. Stuben said in a tone of quiet apology. The old man gave his assent with a stiff nod and they left.

In the carriage again and headed back to Collinwood the young doctor glanced at her and said, "That didn't turn out the way we'd expected it to."

"He made a fool of me!" Diana said bitterly.

"Your story didn't stand up very well."

"But I know he is the one I saw," she protested.

The young doctor was busy at the reins, keeping his eyes on the road ahead. "The fact that Maria is alive and seems better undermines your whole theory."

"Even so, it must have been him who raided that grave!"

"Why not Barnabas?"

She gave the young doctor a frantic glance. "I thought I made it clear about Barnabas. The dead have no interest for him. It is living blood he must have to sustain himself."

"Suppose your story about Barnabas is no more accurate than your theory that the doctor stole the body to transplant Maria's head to it?"

She sat back against the horsehair seat and stared at the rain as they drove along. The drip from the cover of the carriage seemed to symbolize her beaten, dejected mood.

"If you doubt everything I've said, there's not much point in our discussing it," she finally said.

"I'm sorry," the young man said contritely. "I'm not turning against you. But you must admit that scientist, faker or not, put on an excellent show."

"That's all it was! A show!" Diana said angrily. "Wait until I see Barnabas tonight. I'm sure he'll know how to trap that wicked old man."

They had come to the entrance of Collinwood and the doctor brought the carriage to a halt and told her, "I'll expect you to use discretion and not go out alone in the night, exposing yourself to more danger."

"Thank you for your interest," she said coolly.

"I am interested," he said in a firm tone. "I want you to believe that. I need to think this all over." He paused and with a grim smile added, "And in spite of my many reservations, I'll do whatever I can to put in a good word for Barnabas."

"Thank you," she said, hope coming back to her again.

They parted in a friendly mood, though they were both in a state of frustration and puzzled. The forlorn wet day seemed to drag on without end. Towards the evening the rain eased and a heavy fog took over. Diana was impatient to have darkness come so she could go out in search of Barnabas. Under the circumstances he would not come near the house, Stephen having made it plain that he was no longer welcome.

When the family gathered for dinner it was a solemn occasion which seemed to touch even the high spirits of the two younger Collins boys. Jim and his father were mostly silent with grim expressions, and Maude was nervous and unable to maintain any proper conversation. Diana escaped from them as soon as the meal ended.

Since it was already dusk because of the fog, she threw on her cloak and left Collinwood by a side door. She hurried along the path through the heavy mist in the direction of the old house. But when she got there and rapped on the door, there was no answer. She tried several times and had no reply. It was hard to understand. Peters was usually there even when his master was abroad.

At last she gave up. Unhappily, she began walking back towards the main house. She debated what she would do and finally made up her mind to approach the mansion where Dr. Padrel's laboratory was located on her own.

Marching out across the fog-ridden field, she hurried toward the big white mansion. The misty darkness made everything seem different. She wasn't even sure she was walking in the right direction. She recalled Dr. Stuben's warning against venturing out alone at night and began to experience feelings of mounting panic.

Where was she? She stumbled on the rocky ground and realized her shoes were soaked from the tall wet grass. The branches of a tree loomed surprisingly before her. They seemed to reach out like ghostly fingers to touch her. With a small exclamation she wheeled away from their phantom menace.

She must have taken a wrong turn. Yet the way had seemed very direct. It would have been wiser to have remained on the steps of the old house until either Peters or Barnabas had shown up. But it was too late to worry about that now. She groped her way forward, hesitating at each step and knowing she had surely lost her way.

All at once the sound of the ocean was stronger to her ears. The waves seemed to be pounding very close to her. She glanced down and saw to her horror that she was within a step of the edge of the cliff. Another moment and she would have stumbled to her death. She shrank back in apprehension.

It took her a full moment to recover from her fright. But at least now she could work her way back. She knew where the cliffs and danger lay. Collinwood must be in the opposite direction. So she started across the fog-shrouded field again.

Two or three minutes passed before she saw the tiny pinpoint of light through the mist. It seemed to be moving and it was perhaps a hundred yards distant from her. Heartened by the knowledge that there was someone else out walking on this dreadful night she quickened her steps in the direction of the small glowing dot of red.

As she moved closer to the glow of light she recognized it to be a lantern in someone's hand. The gentle swaying motion indicated that. She shouted a greeting to whoever it might be. There was no immediate reply so she called out again as she came within a few feet of the other wanderer in the fog. And then she recognized who it was!

Maria! Maria out on this miserable, mist-ridden night. With a pleased cry of recognition she hurried close to the girl. And then she halted, frozen with fear! For the Maria who stood before her with the tiny red lantern held high in her hand was in no way like the Maria she had known! This creature with mad, burning eyes and an expression of malevolent hatred. The dark hair wildly flowing to the shoulders of the terrifying figure did not cover what Diana's eyes involuntarily sought out!

The jagged line around her neck! The jagged line where flesh had roughly been sewn on flesh and the stitches which still plainly showed. With a wild animal cry the horror came threateningly towards her!

CHAPTER 10

Her hands reached out to open and close on tall wet tufts of grass. She rolled over on one side and moaned. Then, awareness rapidly returning, she opened her eyes wide and gave a frightened cry. The misty darkness was all around her. She sat up and peered into the wraiths of fog with terrified eyes. It seemed only seconds ago the horror of a zombie-like Maria had closed in on her, and now she was alone!

She got to her feet and stood there shakily. Where had the creature gone? Why had it not molested her? They were questions she could not answer. Far off, the foghorn on Collinsport Point droned its monotonous warning. The night was suddenly full of dreadful menace and she could think of nothing but getting back to Collinwood as quickly as she could.

With only a vague idea of where she was heading, she started across the broad field again. She had been terribly wrong to venture out alone. Robert Stuben had warned her against it and she had paid no attention to him. Now she was suffering for her lack of judgment. Even though she'd been lucky enough to escape harm at the hands of the creature which Maria had been transformed into, she couldn't block the nightmare of the encounter from her mind. That nauseating line of stitched flesh around the slim neck of the black-haired girl meant only one thing. Somehow Dr. Padrel had managed to join the dead Maria's head with the body he'd stolen from the grave.

But the thing that had emerged from his operating room was neither of this life or the one beyond the grave. The scientist had turned Maria into a vicious soulless monster!

What would happen now? And where had Barnabas vanished? It was as if the dense fog had swallowed him up. She paused to try and get her bearings. The only thing she could be sure of was that the distant foghorn sounded more faintly at this spot.

She was about to resume walking when she became vaguely aware of a figure moving in the darkness ahead of her. She stood there frozen into a motionless, silent fear as she watched it come towards her and take shape. She had visions of the ghoul-like Maria stalking her again.

But it was not Maria. It was Barnabas who called out to her, "Diana!"

"Yes!" she replied in a voice trembling with relief, and the next moment she was in his arms.

"What are you doing out here alone?" he demanded as he still embraced her.

She was shivering as she pressed tightly to him. "Something awful has happened!" And she began to sob out the details of her terrifying encounter.

Barnabas stared down at her. "Are you certain? Sure that it was Maria? I've just come from Dr. Padrel's and I saw her there."

"You did?" She couldn't believe her ears.

"Yes. He explained she was much better and resting in her room. He allowed me to look in through the doorway and see her in bed. She was sleeping when I was there so I don't know how she could have been here in the field at approximately the same time."

Diana leaned away from him. "It's some sort of trick," she insisted. "Dr. Padrel put on the same show for Dr. Stuben and me earlier in the day. She was in bed sleeping then. She can't have been resting all that time!"

"He mentioned giving her a sedative," Barnabas said.

"There's something wrong! There has to be. Last night he stole the body of that drowned girl from her grave. Surely you know about that."

"I know a body was stolen," Barnabas agreed. "But was it Rudolf Padrel who did it?"

"I saw him going to the cemetery after I left you," she said. "I would have caught up with him, but someone attacked me and tried to strangle me."

Barnabas was frowning. "And yet you came out alone now?"

"I had to see you. Talk to you. Warn you of all the danger

threatening you."

"It seems you're also in danger," he reminded her. "You should have remained at Collinwood. I'd have found some way to reach you."

"Not with Stephen Collins feeling as he does about you," she said. "I was afraid you wouldn't come."

"I can always send Peters with a message."

"We know now that Dr. Padrel is insane and that he has conducted some dreadful experiment with Maria. What did he say to you about your treatment?"

"He gave me my first injection. He seemed very much like his usual self. He even apologized for the way he behaved towards us last night."

"Exactly what he did to Dr. Stuben and me. I'm sure he's playing some kind of evil game. When do you go back to see him?"

"Tomorrow night I get my second injection," Barnabas said. "After that I take two a night. He claims I should be cured within fourteen days."

"I'm sorry," she said. "I don't believe anything he says. And his actions have placed you in a terrible position. The villagers are blaming you for that grave robbery."

"Why should they?"

"They already think you're some kind of phantom and this fits in," she explained. "You should leave while you can."

"I can't," Barnabas said. "Not now that he's started giving me my serum. It may be a small hope but I must cling to it."

"I have no faith in it or him," Diana said unhappily. "I think we should leave at once."

He took her by the arm. "You'll have to trust my judgment," he said. "The treatment is too complicated to take while traveling. I'll have to suffer it out here. I'll take you back to Collinwood."

She said, "Before we go, there's something I must tell you."

His tall, erect figure stood out against the fog. "What?"

"I've had to share your secret with someone."

The man in the caped coat clutched her by the arms. "I depended on you, Diana!"

"And I haven't betrayed you," she promised. "We need a friend who understands and this person can be trusted."

"No one can be trusted with such knowledge," Barnabas warned her. "Who did you tell?"

"Dr. Stuben."

"Stuben!" Barnabas sounded amazed. "Why?"

"He can give us aid. He's a fine man and he's agreed to do what he can."

Barnabas let her go and seemed in a depressed mood. "He

probably thinks you're insane," he said mournfully. "At the best, he may decide you're tricking him with lies."

"He was very reasonable about it. He admitted it was beyond his understanding but he was willing to do what he could.'"

"I'm not happy about it, Diana," Barnabas said in a tense voice.

"It will be all right. I'm sure. And I won't feel so alone. It's awful during the day when I don't dare to try reaching you."

"We'll have to hope it will work out since you've already told him," Barnabas said. "Now let me get you safely home."

The walk through the fog seemed short with the man she loved at her side. In spite of her determination not to build any hopes on the treatment Barnabas was receiving from the mad scientist, she found herself thinking about it. And she knew she was wishing that the serum would be helpful. It had to be. Barnabas was taking such a fearful risk in remaining in Collinsport for that purpose.

They were within sight of Collinwood. Close enough so that in spite of the fog they could see the soft lamplight glowing from several of the windows in the rambling mansion. Barnabas had been silent and thoughtful much of the walk back. Suddenly he halted and uttered a sharp sigh.

Alarmed, she turned to stare up at him. "Barnabas, what is it?"

His handsome face was contorted with pain and he was clutching at his heart. He seemed on the point of collapse. "The serum!" he gasped.

"What about it?" She was terrified.

He shook his head as if to clear his mind. "Too strong!" Then another spasm seemed to vibrate through him and he twisted with pain, the hand still pressed to his heart.

"What has he done to you?" she wailed. "That madman! He's poisoned you on purpose!"

"No!" Barnabas managed this between gritted teeth. His face had lost all color and he dropped down on his knees. "My cane!" he gasped. "Unscrew the head!"

She bent quickly and retrieved his fallen cane. Gripping the stock of it in one hand she tried to unscrew the silver wolf's head with the other. It resisted. "I can't seem to manage it," she cried.

"Must!" he murmured. "Antidote in there! Must have the capsule!"

Diana gave another try. Desperation made this second attempt a success. The silver head came off and she found a secret chamber with a tiny round box in it. She opened the box to discover two yellow capsules. These she slipped into the mouth of Barnabas.

"Swallow them!" she ordered in despair. He seemed too

near a coma to hear her. Too weak to take the capsules. But after a moment she saw him manage to get them down.

She waited, supporting him with her arm. His head was bent now. And then in a surprisingly few seconds he began to come out of the spell. He lifted his head and gave her a grateful glance. After a few more seconds he was able to stand up again. He uttered a deep sigh. "That was close," he said.

She still had the cane shaft in one hand and the silver head in the other. "What did it mean?"

"Padrel warned me and gave me the antidote," Barnabas explained as he took the sections of the cane from her and carefully put them together again. "Part of the serum is distilled fluid from a hawthorn tree. It is very difficult to measure the dosage. A little too much has the same effect on a person with the vampire curse as driving a hawthorn stake through his heart. I might have died without your help."

Diana was shocked by what he'd told her. "The treatment is much too dangerous. Especially with an insane man like Padrel administering it."

Barnabas smiled grimly. "Would anyone but an insane person attempt to cure me?"

She was badly upset. "I still think we should leave here. Tonight if possible."

"Not yet."

"There is something wrong about Maria," she warned. "It will get worse. I know she is dead. He has done some macabre experiment with her."

"I saw her in her bed asleep," Barnabas protested.

As he spoke a terrifying realization came to her. She looked up at him with horror written on her pretty face. "Barnabas!" she whispered.

"What?"

"I've just recalled something."

"Go on."

"When Dr. Stuben and I saw Maria this afternoon the clothes were drawn up high around her. High enough to conceal her throat? Were they pulled up tightly to hide her throat when you saw her tonight?"

He frowned as he attempted to remember. "I'm not sure that I noticed," he said. "It seems to me they were."

"They had to be!" she said excitedly. "That's why he kept her in bed that way. So we wouldn't see the stitches and see where Maria's head had been joined on to that other poor girl's body!"

"You can't be certain about that," Barnabas warned her.

"I know it! I know it!" she said bitterly. "Please listen to me."

"I'll try to discover more when I see Padrel tomorrow night," he told her. "Try to be patient until then."

"We should go back there tonight!" she protested.

"I'm not feeling that well," he confessed. "The capsules helped me some but I'm still very weak."

"He deliberately planned it that way," Diana lamented. "He's so crafty. He wants more time. What will he do next?"

"Whatever he does, we can manage him," Barnabas assured her.

"I only wish I could believe that."

Barnabas took her in his arms and pressed his cold lips to hers. When he let her go he said, "Now, you go on into the house. I'll wait here until I see you safely inside."

"I'll want to see you tomorrow night," she warned Barnabas.

"Let me go for my treatment first," he said. "And I'll find out what I can about Maria. We can meet on the steps of the old house. While you are waiting I'll have Peters watch out for you."

"Goodnight, Barnabas," she said gently. "Take care."

He nodded. She went on to the entrance of the mansion. At the door she hesitated and turned to see him standing there in the fog-shrouded night. She waved to him and he waved in return. Then she went inside.

And a stern Stephen Collins was waiting for her in the hallway. The grim master of Collinwood was plainly in an angry mood. He said in his rasping voice, "You have been with Barnabas just now."

It was a statement, not a question. He must have been watching them from a window. There was no point in denying it. She couldn't see that it would benefit Barnabas.

She said, "Yes, I was with Barnabas."

Stephen eyed her with disdain. "Don't you realize the sort of degenerate he is?"

"I feel sure you are wrong in your opinion of him."

"Not after the day and night I've been through," was the gray-haired man's harsh reply. "I shall never be able to erase this morning from my mind. The sight of that ravaged grave! The coffin open with its lid broken into splinters and the body gone! I have seen terrible things in my time but never such a violation of decency!"

Diana faced the righteous Stephen defiantly. "You have no proof that Barnabas is to blame."

"The whole town knows he's the one responsible," the upset master of Collinwood cried. "He had already established a reputation for lurking about the cemetery. Now he has unleashed new horror on us."

"In what way?"

"Not content with brutally assaulting young women, he has so turned the mind of one of them that she has become a dangerous ghoul like himself. This very night, our housekeeper was badly frightened by some mad girl who came out of the fog and attacked her!"

"Tonight?" Diana asked, thinking about Maria. She guessed it had probably happened just before or after her encounter with the phantom creature.

"This very night, a half-hour ago," Stephen said angrily. "So you must realize what a risk you took being out there. I have nothing against you, but I must forbid your meeting Barnabas while you remain here as my guest."

"But it was Barnabas who brought me here," she protested.

"I felt differently about him then," Stephen explained grimly. "I was willing to give him a second chance in spite of the gossip he inspired during his stay here two years ago. But I know now that I was wrong."

"I'll leave as soon as I can," she said.

"My wife and I, and my son Jim, all have enjoyed your company," the dour, gray-haired man said. "I'm perfectly willing to have you stay just so long as you avoid Barnabas."

"I'm very fond of your cousin," she said.

"After today I can no longer call him cousin."

"I'm sorry," Diana said. "I'll try and find some way out of this."

"No more of this wandering in the dark alone," the master of Collinwood went on. "While you are here I feel it my duty to give you protection. And I expect you to obey my rules."

"I understand," she said quietly, and left him to go upstairs to her bedroom.

It had been a humiliating scene. While she did not blame Stephen Collins for being upset, she thought he was taking a wrong stand. He was too ready to believe Barnabas was the culprit. Instead he should have been looking wider afield. It was amazing that no one had given any attention to Dr. Padrel. He had attracted little attention in Collinsport. Probably because he'd been there such a short time and had been seen out so infrequently.

Barnabas, on the other hand, was well known, and because he roamed about at night in his restless fashion he was getting the blame for everything. She grieved that he had not been willing to leave as she'd suggested. The serum the mad scientist was giving was probably useless in spite of being dangerous. She could see nothing gained by Barnabas staying on. And it was increasingly apparent that she could remain at Collinwood for only a very short time. In this forlorn mood she went to bed.

When she went downstairs in the morning Jim Collins was still at the breakfast table. He rose as she joined him and offered her a knowing smile.

"I hear you received a lecture from my father last night," were his first words.

"How do you know?" she asked.

Jim smiled. "He told my mother and she told me."

"I see."

"Don't let him frighten you. He rarely means half he says. I'm used to his lectures," Jim confided.

"He made his position pretty clear," she said.

"About not wanting you to go on meeting Barnabas."

"Yes."

"I call that good advice."

She lifted her eyebrows. "Unfortunately, it's not advice I can hope to follow."

"You'll be making a mistake," Jim warned her. "By the way, I heard down at the wharf that your other friend, Dr. Padrel, had a visitor arrive on the night boat the night before last."

"Are you sure?" she asked with a frown. She couldn't imagine the scientist having anyone come from Boston to join him.

"Fellow I talked with said he saw this man get off the boat and the doctor came down and met him. They both went away together."

"Did he tell you what the visitor looked like?"

"No. Except to say he was dressed funny. He wore a heavy black suit and had a scarf wrapped around his face so you couldn't see any of it. But that didn't surprise the men on the wharf much; they're expecting to see pretty odd people joining friends of Barnabas. And that Dr. Padrel is a friend of Barnabas."

"So am I," she reminded him quietly.

"You don't count," the young man said.

"Why not?"

"He has you hypnotized or something. Otherwise you're a nice normal kind of girl."

She smiled ruefully. "Don't be too sure. I could be a witch in disguise."

"Seems we have one on the grounds," Jim said. "Some kind of weird female scared the housekeeper half out of her wits last night. The old woman keeps on insisting she saw a ghost with her throat cut all the way around."

"How horrible!"

"Yes," Jim said cheerfully as he got up. "But then, she has a pretty vivid imagination. And it's not much more horrible than what your good friend Barnabas has been up to. Grave robbery is a pretty low sort of crime." Having delivered this opinion, he left her to finish her breakfast alone. She felt little like eating and had nothing much more than tea. It was a fine, warm morning and when she left the dining room she went out to sit in the garden. She'd not been there more than a few minutes when Maude Collins came out to join her. The older woman seated herself on the marble bench beside her.

"I'm sorry Stephen was so rude to you last night," she apologized.

Diana smiled wanly. "He wasn't rude. He just spoke his mind."

"You mustn't worry about what he said," Maude told her. "This grave robbery has him very upset. The girl's parents are naturally distressed and it did happen in our cemetery."

"I know. It was a terrible thing."

"But I don't think Barnabas had anything to do with it," the older woman said. "I'm sure Stephen is wrong in insisting that he did."

"That is my feeling."

"Just give my husband a few days to get over the worst of it."

"I should be leaving anyway."

"Don't rush off on account of what was said last night," Maude insisted. "I'm sure Stephen won't ever mention the matter again."

"I appreciate your kindness," Diana told her.

Maude smiled. "I'm merely being selfish. I so enjoy your being here. Collinwood can be a lonely place."

At that point the older woman's attention was taken by the actions of her two young sons. They were creating a squabble in the barnyard by teasing a deaf old groom. Maude Collins excused herself and hurried off to bring the melee to an end, leaving Diana alone again.

She was not to be alone for long. A few minutes later she saw Dr. Stuben's carriage coming along the road from the village. She left the garden and went out to meet him.

This time he helped her up beside him on the seat of the carriage. He looked very masculine and attractive seated there under the bright sun. He was hatless and wearing a light suit that made him seem more youthful. But his expression was solemn. She at once sensed that there was trouble she hadn't heard about.

"What is it?" she asked.

He eyed her speculatively. "Why do you begin that way?"

"I'm sure something has gone wrong."

"A pretty good guess," he said grimly.

"Is it about Barnabas?"

"Indirectly."

"Please don't make a mystery of it," she begged.

The young doctor glanced away. "It isn't the easiest thing to talk about," he said. "There's no nice way to tell you."

"Just tell me!"

He looked at her, his eyes troubled. "Something washed up on the beach this morning near the fish packing plant."

"Yes?"

"Something mightily unpleasant." He paused. "The head of that girl whose body was stolen from her grave. It had been roughly cut from her body and tossed in the ocean."

"Oh, no!" she gasped, and raised the back of her hand to cover her mouth.

"Don't faint on me," he said, placing an arm around her.

She shook her head. "No. I'll be all right."

"So it begins to look as if our mad friend, Padrel, tried out his head transplant after all. He deceived us neatly yesterday morning. But this changes everything."

She looked at him. "Last night a thing attacked me in the fog. It was Maria! I could see the stitches where her head was attached to the other body. Later she frightened the housekeeper here."

"Have you talked to Barnabas?"

"Yes."

"What does he think?"

"He's not sure. Dr. Padrel let him see Maria just as he allowed us to look through the doorway at her. But in addition to that the scientist has begun to give Barnabas his treatments. He had the first one last night."

"Barnabas should leave here quickly," the young doctor said. "The villagers were up in arms about him before. After that head being found this morning they're apt to do anything."

"I know," she said, her eyes full of fear. "And Barnabas plans to remain here for two weeks more until he finishes taking the serum treatments from Dr. Padrel."

"He mustn't! Especially since Padrel is probably leading him on again to get money from him. There'll be no cure!"

"That's what I think," she agreed. "What can we do?"

"Try to make Barnabas see things as we see them," was the young doctor's opinion. "Of course we won't be able to talk to him until tonight."

"Not until after sundown."

"Doesn't he have a servant looking after him?" he asked.

"Yes. Peters."

"Suppose we drive over and speak with him. I can leave a message for your stubborn friend Barnabas. I think we should all meet tonight and try and find out exactly what Padrel has been up to."

"I agree," she said.

"Very well," the young doctor said. "We'll drive over to the old house."

It took only a few minutes by horse and carriage. Diana felt this might be an excellent move. They had just passed the barns when they got their first glimpse of the old house and saw the group of people standing in front of it. The crowd seemed to be all male and there was a hint of tension about them even at a distance. They were pointing to the house excitedly and others were coming up to join the cluster every minute.

Dr. Stuben halted the carriage and stared ahead grimly. "Looks as if we've arrived too late," he said. "That's a mob come to pay a visit on Barnabas!"

CHAPTER 11

"Oh, no!" she exclaimed in dismay, knowing he was right.

"I don't know how best to handle this," he murmured as if he were debating with himself. "Barnabas wouldn't listen and now it is very late indeed."

"They'll destroy him if they find him!" she said tearfully.

"Where is he?"

"Somewhere in the cellar. I've never been down there. Peters said he had a room especially prepared for his daytime sleeping."

Dr. Stuben gave her an odd look. "He spends his days in a coffin, doesn't he? I've been doing some catching up on my vampire reading."

"Yes. In a coffin. Usually with a candle lit by its head. He won't be able to do anything. He'll be at their mercy!"

"So it seems!" the young doctor said, studying the growing crowd before the old house. "They're using the back road. That's why you didn't notice them from Collinwood."

Diana suddenly had a last desperate hope. "If we drove to the factory and brought Stephen Collins back, he could stop them. They respect him and would listen to him."

The young man kept watching the crowd of angry, gesticulating men swarming towards the entrance of the old house. "We haven't time," was his opinion. "And anyway, I think it would take more than Stephen to stop that crowd now."

"They're insane! Going after the wrong person!"

"It's happened a few times before, if you're familiar with your history books. They're ignorant, frightened and angry. That's a pretty nasty combination. And it's liable to explode any minute now."

Diana turned in the seat and pleaded, "We'll have to try and do something!"

She pictured Barnabas asleep in his coffin somewhere in the murky depths of the cellar. He would have no hint of the wild storm breaking around him. If the crowd became bold enough to burst into the house they would search every part of it until they found him. He would have no chance to defend himself as they attacked him like a pack of angry wolves.

"Look!" he said sharply.

She did and saw that Peters had opened the door and come out on the top step to try and placate the milling group gathered before the old house. She said, "That poor little man won't be able to turn them back!"

"At least he's trying," Robert Stuben said grimly. "We can't do less." And he flicked the reins and sent the horse along at a fast jog. It took them only a few minutes to reach the edge of the crowd. He gave her the reins to keep the uneasy horse in check while he jumped down from the carriage and made his way to the steps beside Peters.

Diana watched tensely as the young doctor lifted an arm to catch the crowd's attention and then pleaded with them to disperse and let the law take whatever action was necessary. He pointed out that Barnabas probably had nothing to do with the grave robbery. That nothing had been proven. But she could see his words were making little impact on the sullen crowd.

A wave of angry murmuring mounted and they advanced on the steps, sweeping both Peters and the young doctor aside. In the next moment they were pouring into the house. Diana's eyes brimmed with frightened tears.

A disheveled Robert Stuben came back to the side of the carriage. "I'm going to stay, but I think you'd better get away from here."

"No!" she protested.

"It's best," he insisted. "I don't know what horror is coming next. You love Barnabas. It isn't right for you to stay. I may be able to help him."

"My place is with him!"

"Go back to Collinwood and wait for me there!" he said with firm authority and he swung the head of the horse around and gave it a slap on the flank to send it trotting off in the direction of the main house.

Diana sobbed as she tried to bring the frightened horse under control again. The doctor had accomplished what he wanted without further argument. By the time she reached the front entrance of Collinwood she was able to halt the nervous animal.

Almost as soon as she got there Maude came hurrying out the front door to join her. The older woman looked shocked.

"What is happening at the old house? I looked out one of the upper windows and saw the crowd."

"Some of the village men have come for Barnabas," Diana said brokenly. "They blame him for robbing that grave."

"They came by the back road!" Maude said. "Otherwise we would have seen them before this. I'll send word down to the factory. Stephen will soon put an end to this nonsense."

"I'm afraid it's too late. They've already gone into the house looking for Barnabas."

"Poor Barnabas!" Maude said. "I've never believed him guilty of half the things he's been accused of."

"I know he's innocent," Diana told her as she still sat in the carriage, holding the reins.

Maude seemed to finally be aware that this was the doctor's carriage. "Where is Dr. Stuben?"

"Back there, trying to help Barnabas."

"He's a fine young man," the mistress of Collinwood said. "I'm going to have one of the stable boys let Stephen know what is going on." She left Diana to hurry around the house to the stables.

Diana was tom between a desire to drive back to the old house and see what was developing and fear of what she might find there. Dr. Stuben had ordered her to wait where she was and probably he was right. She closed her eyes and prayed for the safety of Barnabas.

Perhaps ten minutes had gone by before the first of the many farm wagons came rattling past the lawns of Collinwood on their way back to the village. Though they had used the little-traveled back road to gather in secrecy, they were being bolder in leaving. No need to hide themselves now that their mission had been accomplished. She watched the wagons go by, noting the stern faces of the men in them. And as the dust rolled from their clattering great wheels she saw the last one come along. When it was almost opposite her it stopped and a slim figure jumped down from it.

The wagon went on and Dr. Stuben hurried across to the carriage. He was perspiring but he looked less tense as he swung up onto the seat beside her.

"The news is good," he said.

"Good?" she questioned with a tremor in her voice. "How

could it be?"

"They didn't find him."

"But he had to be there!"

"He wasn't. They searched the house from top to bottom. I was down in the cellar when they burst the door of that hidden room. It was empty!"

"Peters said that was where he spent his days."

"Peters vanished. I wasn't able to speak to him. I don't know where Barnabas is but they certainly didn't find him."

She gave a deep sigh of relief. "At least he's safe for a little."

"We can assume so," the young doctor agreed. "But those people are in a bad mood. They're going to keep on looking for him. If he shows himself in or around the village they'll tear him apart."

"He must be made to leave," she agreed.

"You're probably the only one who can convince him to do that," the doctor said.

"I'm not sure he'll listen to me. That awful Dr. Padrel seems to have some power over him."

"It's the strong desire Barnabas has to be cured," Dr. Stuben said. "His desperation makes him an easy victim for a charlatan of that man's type."

"Are you going to visit Dr. Padrel and find out something of what happened to Maria?"

"Not now. I can't. I've given more time than I can afford to this. I do have patients who need my care."

"I'm sorry," she said contritely. "I'd forgotten."

"I'll come back tonight if I can manage it," he said. "It all depends on the calls on me. I would like to talk to Barnabas and also try and find out what mad thing Padrel has done to Maria."

Memory of the horror of seeing the zombie-like girl registered on Diana's pretty face. "I'm sure he did that gruesome operation and that she is now mad."

"Small wonder," he said grimly. Then he took the reins from her. "I must be going."

"Thank you for all you've done," she said, studying his tanned, pleasant young face.

He shrugged. "I still find it hard to believe. But I'll continue to help in any way I can. Meanwhile, I'll expect you to be cautious. That's more important now than ever before."

"I know," she said.

He helped her down from the carriage and then drove off just as Maude came back from the stables. The older woman glanced after the vanishing carriage and then gave Diana a questioning look.

"What happened?"

"They didn't find Barnabas!"

"Praise be for that," the mistress of Collinwood said fervently. "I've sent a boy to the factory. Stephen should soon be here."

Diana said, "I have no idea where Barnabas may have gone. I don't believe he would leave Collinwood without telling me. When we talked last night he said he was going to remain here."

"Barnabas isn't a fool," Maude said. "After the trouble started two years ago he left in the night. He may have decided it was best to do that this time."

"But he'd somehow get word to me," Diana protested, faced with a new worry now. "He'd leave a message with Peters if nothing else."

"You haven't had a chance to talk with Peters yet."

"No."

"Maybe he will have word for you."

Diana nodded. "It's possible." But none of it made sense to her. Maude Collins did not know that Barnabas was a vampire who would not travel without someone like Peters to take care of him during his daylight resting period. There had to be some other answer and she believed the answer must lie in the old house.

She said, "I'm going to walk back to the old house and see if Peters has returned."

The older woman showed alarm. "Some of those men may still be there. It may not be safe. Don't you think it would be better to wait until Stephen gets here? Then you could go together."

"I don't want to wait," Diana said uneasily. "You can tell him where I've gone."

"Do be careful!" Maude called after her.

Diana was already heading for the path that led by the barns to the original Collinwood. Her thoughts were confused and troubled. She had to find out where Barnabas was and try and reason with him. Make him understand that she loved him and was willing to marry him even if he never recovered from the dark curse that was shadowing his life.

Ahead she saw the old house looking somber and deserted. The crowd had all gone. There wasn't anyone in sight. As she came nearer she saw that the front door was still open. She went up the steps and inside. Only then in the cool shadows of the hallway was she aware of the tide of anger that had surged through the ancient house.

Tables were overturned, ornaments lay broken on the floor, even the tapestries and paintings had been torn from the walls. The house which Stephen had so carefully restored was a shambles. She moved through the ruins with a look of incredulity on her attractive face. It was hard to believe the violence of the crowd.

A tour of the upper sections of the building gave no clue to where Barnabas or Peters might be. So she decided on a brief search of the cellar. She knew it could be hazardous but she felt that she might find the answer she was looking for down there. She kept telling herself there could be a secret room which the angry mob had overlooked. And in it she might find the coffin of Barnabas with Peters guarding it.

With this thought to bolster her courage, she bent down and retrieved a broken candle from a twisted candelabra on the living room floor. Finding a match, she lit the candle and slowly approached the door leading to the cellar. It was also open. She had never been down there before.

The odor of dampness and decay assailed her nostrils as she started down the steep stone steps. As she went lower the shadows gathered around her until she was in complete darkness. This was like another eerie world.

The candle she was holding flickered weakly and she felt a pang of fear as she thought it was going out. But the flame revived and she went slowly forward along the length of the gloomy underground place. It was almost cold, clammy cold! And it was very silent. Strange objects loomed around her, great packing cases and other stored items that took on a ghostly appearance in the thick shadows.

There were things scattered on the hard earthen floor of the cellar as evidence that the raging crowd had been down there as well. Then, directly in front of her, she saw an open door. It led to a room beyond and she guessed this must be the room where Barnabas had normally spent his days. She continued on through the doorway and held the candle high to inspect the room.

It was cell-like with nothing on its walls and floor.

There were no windows and no sign of furniture. Yet she had the feeling this had been the place. She wondered if there might be still another hidden room off it but could see no evidence of a secret door. After a moment spent carefully inspecting the walls and floor for any suspicious crevices to indicate a concealed entrance, she decided to give up.

Turning, she started out of the room. But she only took one step and then the ghastly thing loomed up before her—the mad horror that Maria Padrel had become! The disheveled black hair, the insane eyes and the crudely stitched neck filled Diana with terror. The phantom creature in a dirty white flowing gown stretched her hands out and gave an eerie shriek of laughter.

Diana felt the hands touch her! They were cold and wet! With a wild scream of her own, she dropped the candle and was left in the darkness with the loathsome zombie! She pushed by

Maria and ran stumbling along the length of the cellar blindly, with peals of mad laughter following her. She found the stone steps and sobbingly groped her way up them to the less shadowed hall above.

A stern figure stood in the hall to greet her. It was the gray-haired Stephen Collins, who regarded her with a look of extreme distaste on his aristocratic features.

"What does this mean?" he demanded, apparently outraged by her tears and screams.

In the face of his severity she partly recovered herself. Pointing to the cellar steps, she said, "Down there! I saw a phantom!"

Stephen Collins eyed her grimly. "Did you see Barnabas?"

"No. But there is something down there."

The master of Collinwood scowled. "It is odd that I have never encountered any of the ghosts that are supposed to haunt the estate. I think we may put your experience down to overwrought nerves."

"I did see someone," she insisted. "A girl in a flowing white robe."

Stephen looked even more annoyed. "Very well," he said. "I'll go down and look for myself."

He left her and rummaged for a candle in the mess of the ruined house. When he had one he stalked by her without a glance and went down the steps into the blackness of the cellar. She waited, nerves on edge, expecting at any moment to hear Maria's screams or some cry of horror and surprise from Stephen. But no sound came. And after a short time the austere man came up the steps again with an angry gleam in his eyes.

"There is no sign of anyone down there," he told her accusingly.

"Then she must have somehow gotten out!" she protested.

"How?" he demanded. "The only other exit is locked."

She stood there in bewilderment and dejection. "I don't know."

"This house!" the gray-haired man raged as he strode to the living room door and glanced in. "See what those ignorant village louts have done to it. I'll make them pay for damaging my property in this fashion."

"Dr. Stuben tried to stop them," she said. "They wouldn't listen."

Stephen glared at her. "Barnabas is to blame for all this. I should never have allowed him to return."

"I think you are wrong," she protested.

Stephen ignored her remark. In a cold voice, he asked, "Are you returning to Collinwood with me?"

"No. I'll wait here a little."

"Not in this house," he said firmly. "I would not think of exposing you to more phantoms." This was said with sarcasm. "I'm going to put a padlock on the door until I can send someone to begin repairing this damage."

"I was going outside anyway," she said faintly, and slowly made her way to the door and into the sunshine.

As she didn't want to talk to him, she walked away from the house with her back towards Collinwood. And this led her across the field in the direction of the cemetery. When she saw where she was going, something made her continue on as if an inner voice were guiding her until at last she slowly entered the cemetery gates.

It was shaded, peaceful and rather lovely in a somber way in this haven of the dead. It came to her that if Barnabas had not been changed from a normal human to a vampire, his bones would be resting in this quiet place now. Perhaps he would have lived, loved and died without anyone remembering his name. But the curse had changed all that. Angelique in her diabolical revenge had sentenced him to long years of phantom wandering.

Now Diana wanted to somehow give this handsome, tortured man a taste of happiness, but fate seemed to be laughing at their love. And so Barnabas was in this dreadful trouble and she had no idea where he might have vanished. She moved on past the green mounds marking the graves and the headstones of various shapes and sizes. Most of the buried were of the Collins name. She went deeper into the realm of the dead, noting the inscriptions on the stones until she had reached the section of the cemetery bordering on the tall forest.

She was bent studying an ancient gray stone whose inscription was badly blurred by the weathering of long years when she heard an odd rustling sound from behind her.

Then her name was whispered, "Miss Diana!"

She whirled around to discover Peters standing there. The little man pressed a finger to his lips to ensure her silence. Then in a low voice, he asked, "Are you here alone?"

"Yes."

"Very good," the little man said. "I thought you were, so I decided to take a chance. I wanted to let you know Mr. Barnabas is safe."

She gave a deep sigh of relief. "I've been hoping I'd find you."

"I had to be careful," Peters said. "The Master wanted me to remain at the house as long as possible to confuse the mob."

"You did very well. Where is he?"

The little man glanced around cautiously and then leaned close to her. "He is here."

"In the cemetery?"

"What better place?" Peters wanted to know. "It was the Master decided. Towards the dawn we brought his coffin down here and put it in one of the tombs of the family. He is in there now."

"At least he's safe for the moment, but he must leave when darkness comes."

Peters looked dejected. "I don't know about that, miss. He's very anxious for Dr. Padrel to continue giving him that serum."

"I don't trust that charlatan," she said angrily.

"I'm on your side in that, miss," the little man said in a sad voice. "But he has convinced Mr. Barnabas he can cure him."

Diana glanced at Peters. "May I see Barnabas for a moment?"

Peters hesitated. "I don't know, miss. Have you ever seen him at rest before?"

"No," she confessed. "But it would give me comfort to be with him. If only for a moment."

The servant looked uncertain. Then he seemed to make up his mind. "Very well," he said. "I'll show you the way."

She followed him a short distance to a large black marble vault with the name Collins boldly on it. The iron door to the underground tomb was padlocked. Peters drew a large rusted key from his pocket and struggled with the huge padlock until it creaked open. Then he pushed open the iron door. It scraped on the stone floor and a pungent odor of death and decay was released. Peters gave her a solemn look over his shoulder and led the way into the tomb.

There were only two steps down to the level of the inner room. As her eyes became accustomed to the shadowed place she saw the shelves on either side with their dusty, cobwebbed caskets. At the very rear of the tomb there was the familiar coffin Barnabas had shown her that night in Italy. Her heart began to pound in excitement, since she knew he was in it.

Peters whispered, "I have kept the coffin closed today, just in case."

"Of course," she agreed. "It is safer."

The little man carefully opened the upper section of the casket top and she saw Barnabas placidly resting there. His melancholy, handsome face had the true corpselike look as he lay there motionless with his eyes closed. The pallor of his skin completed the illusion. His powerful hands were neatly folded. Overwhelmed by her love for him, she bent down and touched her lips to his cold forehead.

Somehow he would know she was there. She was sure of that. In that other world to which he retreated during these daytime hours he must still have knowledge of what was happening in the realm of the living. Then she stood back and allowed Peters to close the coffin lid.

Nothing was said between them until they had left the tomb and Peters had carefully locked it again. They walked a distance away and she then told the little man, "I must see Barnabas as soon as he awakes."

Peters looked worried. "Don't come here, miss."

"But where? Stephen has locked up the old house."

The little man frowned. "I'd be afraid of someone following you here. It could be very bad for the Master."

"I know," she agreed. "We must keep this retreat a secret."

"It would be better if he came to you," Peters said.

"Not at Collinwood. He can't meet me there."

"Widows' Hill," Peters said. "When it is finally dark go there and wait. I will see that he comes to you."

She studied the little man with troubled eyes. "You're sure that will be best?"

"Yes, miss."

Diana felt it would be pointless to argue. She told him she would wait for Barnabas at the lonely point along the cliffs. Then she said goodbye to him and hurried from the cemetery. She looked to see if there was anyone around, but the field and the general area near the cemetery were completely deserted.

More confident, she began to walk back to Collinwood. At least Barnabas was safe and she'd been with him a moment. But as she neared the grim, locked old house she remembered the phantom she'd so recently encountered in its dark cellar. How had Maria gotten down there and where had she vanished? Stephen Collins had not taken time to search the cellar carefully, so the mad zombie-like thing Maria had become might still be lurking there in the shadows.

She increased her pace and hurried by the old house as quickly as she could. She knew that as long as the phantom Maria was at large, the village would continue to be terrorized. And that meant things would grow continually worse for Barnabas. He would be blamed for all the evil the mad scientist and his monstrous creation perpetrated.

Dr. Stuben had promised he would return in the evening if his patients allowed him. She hoped that he would. It seemed to her if she, the doctor, and Barnabas could hold a short meeting together they might be able to plan some way out of the dreadful web of circumstances. The thing complicating any sensible action was the faith Barnabas had that Dr. Padrel with his serum would be able to cure him this time. It was a faith she felt wasn't warranted.

She reached Collinwood and went inside. Jim Collins was

in the hallway and when he saw her a smirk came over his youthful face. "I was just going to look for you," he said.

"Were you?"

"Yes. Mother was worried about you. And you have a visitor."

"A visitor?"

He nodded with a mocking gleam in his eyes. "He's waiting for you in the living room."

Diana was startled. She couldn't imagine who it might be or why Jim was making such a mystery of it. Not wanting him to realize she was upset, she attempted a casual air and said, "Then I mustn't keep him waiting any longer."

She left the young man and rather hesitantly entered the big living room. Seated there in a high-backed chair was Dr. Padrel. She couldn't help staring at him in some amazement since he was about the last person she'd ever expected to have coming calling on her.

"Dr. Padrel," she said. "I was told you were waiting for me."

Dr. Padrel rose stiffly, gazing at her malevolently. "Yes," he said. "I have come to give you a message. A message I want you to pass on to Barnabas Collins."

She was at once cautious. "If I happen to see him."

"You will see him," the scientist assured her. "And when you do, tell him the experiment is over. I will not continue treating him with the serum."

CHAPTER 12

The doctor's words left Diana at a complete loss. The shock of his unexpected appearance was doubled by this abrupt announcement. It was contrary to all she had expected of him. And she could only surmise that it was a new twist in a wily scheme to victimize Barnabas.

She said, "Isn't this rather a sudden decision?"

The puffy face of the sinister Padrel revealed a gloating look. He said, "Mr. Barnabas Collins has had it his own way long enough. He has chosen to cast aside my daughter in favor of you. So I am denying him the serum."

"But you knew about Barnabas and me from the time we met in Italy," she pointed out.

"Only when Maria became ill did I realize the harm Barnabas Collins had done to her."

"Barnabas did nothing more than try to be nice to her."

The man's eyes narrowed. "We both know how the situation stands. You can tell him that is my final word."

"He will want to see you himself."

Dr. Padrel shrugged. "It will do him no good. Unless he wants to change his mind and marry Maria."

Diana gave him a searching look. "Is Maria well enough to be married?" Memory of the demented creature she had encountered in the cellar still haunted her. She began to think it could be the chagrin the mad scientist felt at the failure of his experiment that was making him take this stand now.

"Maria would make a good enough wife for Barnabas Collins. Without my serum he has not much to offer a bride," the doctor said with a sneer.

"I think you are taking out your failure to successfully revive Maria on Barnabas," she said. "But I'll be frank and say I would rather have him as he is than see him under your control."

The puffy face took on an evil smile. "Then my decision should satisfy you."

"It's more important that it should satisfy Barnabas," she told him evenly. "He has gone to great effort and expense in bringing you here and you have repaid him by placing him under the gravest suspicion."

"Indeed?"

"I know it was you who stole the body of that poor girl from her grave and who mutilated it in your clumsy attempt to restore Maria to life."

Dr. Padrel eyed her coldly. "May I say your statements are utterly mad."

"I think not," she said sharply. "The discovery of that girl's severed head on the beach caused some of the villagers to come out here and vandalize the house Barnabas has been occupying. It is only a miracle that they did not destroy him."

"If you'll forgive me," Dr. Padrel said, "I'm not interested. I'll say good day, Miss Hastings." With a formal bow he walked past her and out to the hallway.

She made no attempt to follow him and show him out politely. She felt such loathing and contempt for the charlatan that she hoped never to see him again. She was sure he had some wicked plan in mind. This denial of the serum to Barnabas was for a purpose. Perhaps the explanation was as simple as his merely knowing the serum wouldn't work. This was his way to squirm out of the bargain.

While she knew Barnabas would be severely disappointed, she felt it could be for the best. There would be no reason for the man she loved to remain in Collinsport with the hope of a cure by the sinister doctor ruled out. Perhaps she might now be able to persuade Barnabas to escape with her to a safer climate. It was the only solution.

But she would not be able to see him until after dark. And then only when he chose to show himself at Widows' Hill. It was to be a period of anxious waiting.

The day wore on and her tension mounted. Stephen Collins

sent workmen from the plant to begin clearing up most of the mess at the old house. And he sent Jim back to supervise them. After staying on the job for a little the brash young man returned to Collinwood and began taunting Diana.

Finding her seated in the garden, he asked, "What happened to your gentleman friend?"

She looked at him indignantly. "I don't intend to notice that question."

"Then you don't know where Barnabas is?"

"Why should I?"

He looked grimly amused. "I thought you two were very much in love. Don't lovers keep better track of each other?"

"That's not any of your business," she turned her back on him and studied a bed of colorful mixed blooms.

He sat down on the bench beside her. "Why not make it out of sight and out of mind and begin to take an interest in a real man!"

She glanced at him with a bitter smile. "Meaning you?"

"Why not?"

"Because I see you as a mere boy. A bundle of sullen immaturity."

Jim frowned. "I can offer you more than crazy Barnabas."

"You shouldn't call him that."

"My father says he is insane. Look at the damage he caused at the old house! Isn't that proof enough for you?"

"The villagers were the ones who vandalized the place."

"He made them do it."

"I disagree," she said.

"You disagree with anything but the kindliest views of Barnabas. All the rest of us consider him a menace."

"Then it is something on which we are not likely ever to agree," she suggested quietly.

This apparently was enough to make Jim cease tormenting her. He left the garden and went back to his duties of overseeing the cleaning up of the old house. Meanwhile she worried about the evening ahead, and wondered if Dr. Stuben would manage to find time to see her as he'd promised, providing his patients didn't keep him too busy. She prayed that he would. She urgently needed his help and advice now.

When dusk fell she left Collinwood and walked to Widows' Hill. Jim had asked her where she was going and she had to be abrupt with him to discourage his going with her. This was the last thing she wanted. It was a warm, clear night with no hint of fog. By the time she reached the high point above the cliffs it was dark.

Far down below, the waves washed greedily on the beach. The sky was dark without stars. It was destined to be one of those black nights when there would be no moonlight. She waited there with bated breath, hoping each moment would bring Barnabas to her. But the minutes went by and he did not come. It seemed she must have been there more than a half-hour. Glancing back towards Collinwood, she could see lights in the ground floor windows of the rambling big house.

She hoped this would be her last night at Collinwood—that Barnabas would agree to leave and she could go with iiim. The tragic and frightening events of the past week had turned her completely against the place. The more distance she could place between herself and the malevolent scientist the better she would be pleased.

There was a footstep close to her and then she saw the vague outline of the caped figure of Barnabas. He came up to her and said, "I hope I haven't kept you waiting too long."

"What does it matter after all that has happened? I'm satisfied to know you are safe," she said with deep emotion.

"It was a close thing," Barnabas agreed. And he took her in his arms and kissed her. But there was a strangeness about him. A suggestion of despair.

As he released her, she said, "I have a message for you from Dr. Padrel."

He nodded moodily. "I know all about it. I have just come from there."

She was surprised. "You have?"

"He gave me his ultimatum. Either I marry Maria or he withdraws the serum."

"I'm sure the serum is worthless in any event."

Barnabas frowned. "I wonder."

"If he thought it had any chance of success, he wouldn't use this excuse to break his part of the agreement."

"I think it is because he is concerned about Maria. He wouldn't allow me to see her tonight. And I believe your theory about her is correct. He went through with this macabre operation and she is alive but mad."

"The thing to do is leave at once," she urged. "Peters can find a carriage and prepare your coffin. I'll get a few things and join you."

Barnabas gave her a bitter glance. "I can't allow you to think of anything like that. It's bad enough that I'm a vampire. But now I'll be hunted as a madman."

"The turmoil will die down once you're away from here," she insisted.

"I'm not ready to go yet."

"But there's nothing to keep you here now," she said. "Unless you want to accept that evil scientist's terms and marry Maria."

"That's out of the question," Barnabas said. "But I feel there is still a chance I may be able to bargain with him. This could all be a trick to get more money from me."

"If you can see that, you must be able to see that his serum is worthless."

"Hope dies hard."

"So it seems," she said. "You know how close a call you had this morning. Every hour you remain in Collinsport you are in more danger. What do you propose to do?"

"I'll wait at least one more night," he said. "I may be able to get around Padrel yet."

"He's no good!" she protested.

But Barnabas was plainly not going to listen to her. Taking her by the arm, he said, "I'll see you safely back to Collinwood."

And he did. He left her a dozen yards from the front door and kissed her goodnight again, promising to meet her at the same place the following night. She listened to him dully, much of her hope lost, and then went on into the house.

Maude came down the stairs to greet her. "Someone came with a message for you just after you left," she said.

"Oh?"

The older woman handed her a sealed envelope. "I waited up to give it to you," she said with a sympathetic smile. "I thought it might be from Barnabas."

"I doubt that," she said, taking the envelope. "Thank you, anyway."

When the older woman returned upstairs Diana opened the envelope and read the message enclosed as she stood there in the hallway. The message was terse and in a crabbed hand. It said: "Must see you at once. Possible we can arrange something regarding the cure for Barnabas." It was signed by Dr. Padrel.

Diana scanned the short message twice. Her instant reaction was that the scheme was beginning to unwind. Whatever the crafty scientist was up to would soon be revealed to them. She disliked the idea of going back to the old white mansion but she had little choice. Her curiosity and the desire to get whatever information she could for Barnabas made it imperative that she obey the summons, though she was sure both Barnabas and Dr. Stuben would be dead set against her doing so. But neither of them were on hand to be consulted, so the decision must be hers. And her decision was to face the demented scientist and try to discover what evil game he was playing.

She quietly let herself out of the house and began hurrying across the lawn in the dark. The black night was a perfect one for phantoms, and she was pursued by the horror of her encounters with the transformed Maria. Fear gave her passage through the night wings. Within an incredibly short time she saw the lights of the big white mansion. She reached the front door and rapped on it.

Dr. Padrel opened the door almost at once. His puffy face smiled cunningly. "So you decided to come?"

"Why not?" she asked, pretending courage she didn't feel.

"Indeed, why not," he said, standing back for her to enter.

She did, and stood there in the dull light of the hall. "What was it you wanted to discuss with me?"

"We'll get to that in a moment," he said. "If you'll just come down the hall we'll be able to talk in complete privacy. And this is a most delicate matter. I'm sure you'll agree."

"I see no reason why we can't talk about it here," she said, not anxious to leave the comparative safety of the front hall.

"I must insist," he said firmly, his pale eyes meeting hers. "I have personal reasons for the request. Maria is in the house. I do not want her to overhear us."

Diana hesitated. It seemed a modest request. So she said, "Very well," and followed him down the long hall to the part of the mansion fronting on the ocean.

He stopped before a door at the end of the hall and opened it. "In there," he said.

She stepped inside, expecting him to follow. But he didn't. Instead he closed the door, leaving her in almost complete darkness. She turned and tried the door and found it was locked. He had tricked her into being trapped in this dark room. Why? As her eyes became adjusted to the shadows she tried to make out what sort of place it was.

And then she heard a slight movement from a distant corner. Her nerves went on edge as she pressed back against the door with her eyes widening in terror. What horror lurked in that room with her? The sound came again and then there was a low chuckle from someone in the corner.

A match was struck and touched to a candle and she saw who her companion in the room was. She couldn't believe it! It was like a nightmare being piled on top of a nightmare. She studied the leering, ugly figure holding the candle and gradually coming nearer her.

"No!" she whispered in growing panic.

"Yes!" The reply came with grating satisfaction.

"Not you!"

"Sorry to disappoint you, Miss Hastings. Your friend Barnabas didn't kill me, though I must say he made an excellent try." The menacing figure ended this statement with a high-pitched giggle, for it was the Count of Baraga.

She gazed at the reptilian face in fear and asked, "How did you know where I was?"

"You were not hard to trace and Dr. Padrel is an old acquaintance of mine. He owed me a slight favor and so was very willing to have me as a house guest. I arrived here several nights ago on the night boat."

"What do you want?"

"We'll get to that," he said. "First, let me tell you that your friend Barnabas need never hope for a cure at the hands of Dr. Padrel. He is no doctor, and no scientist. He is a rather shoddy charlatan."

"I'd already decided that," she told him.

The Count held the candle close to her and with a grin on his ugly face went on. "Since my arrival I've taken charge of things here. To prove I'm not the simple idiot you may have taken me to be back in Palermo let me say that it was my idea to have the grave robbed, knowing it would incense the villagers against an already suspected Barnabas Collins."

"I knew I saw Dr. Padrel with the shovel."

"You did, indeed," the Count said with another of his weird giggles. "And it was I who tutored Maria in her role of monster and drew that jagged stitch line around her throat."

"No!" she gasped.

"It seemed very real, didn't it?" the Count said triumphantly. "And I consider Maria an excellent actress. I've assured her that she shall have a career on the stage. I have some influence with eminent theater persons. I also arranged for the girl's body to be mutilated and her head found on the beach. That was the crowning touch, don't you agree?"

"Why indulge in such degeneracy?"

"To be sure that Barnabas Collins would be recognized as the vampire and demon that he is!" the Count snapped.

"But Barnabas is a fine man. Not at all like that. He is an unfortunate victim of his condition."

"The people of Collinsport think differently," the Count said with cold amusement. "And they will finish Barnabas without bothering to discover the truth. Unless you want to save him."

"Is this another of your insane jokes?"

"I assure you it is no joke for you," the Count of Baraga said. "You have a choice. You can agree to marry me and I promise there will be no more charades to place Barnabas in a bad position. Or you can refuse and meet a violent death here. A death for which I will make sure Barnabas is blamed."

"How can you possibly do that?"

"More easily than you think," the ugly Count of Baraga told her. And he left her to go to the center of the room and lift up a trap door. A yawning opening was revealed. Now he returned and seized her arm roughly, saying, "Come. I will show you."

She had no choice. His grip was like steel. He pushed her ahead of him as they went down a flight of stone steps. Then they were in a low passage of some sort. Still maneuvering her on ahead of him he led her through the darkness to what she recognized as the mouth of a cave. A cave in the face of the cliff at least a hundred feet above the rocky beach. She recalled Barnabas telling her about this underground passage that had been constructed between the white mansion and the cliffs.

"Look down, my dear," the Count said with a giggle. "I guarantee it will make you dizzy." As he spoke he picked up a pine torch and touched the candle to it.

Instantly it lit up and in its ruddy glow she had a much better view of both him and her surroundings. He was dressed in a black suit that did not flatter his stooped figure, and he looked as mad and menacing as he had back in his own castle.

"This is insanity," she pleaded. "I will never marry you. You've done all the harm you can do to Barnabas. I'm not afraid of you. You must let me go."

Holding the torch at shoulder level he came close to her, his eyes bright with madness. "When you leave here it will be as my fiancee or as a broken body down on the rocks. I'll give you a few minutes to make up your mind."

She saw how it would end. When she further enraged him with her refusal he would nudge her with the flaming pine torch until she toppled down from the mouth of the cave. And when her body was found, Barnabas would be blamed once again. The Count would arrange that. She had no doubt he would even arrange some suitable vampire mark on the throat of her dead body to be sure.

"Well, Miss Hastings?" The Count came a step nearer, the torch thrust so close to her she could feel its burning heat. She backed just a little. In a moment she would be at the edge and then over.

From the black sky there came the sound of fluttering wings and in the next instant a giant bat-like creature came into the mouth of the cave and winged directly towards the Count. He screamed in his high-pitched voice and stumbled back using the torch to fend off the frightening denizen of the night.

In a split second the bat became Barnabas. The Count gave a howl of anger and whipped out a pistol. He fired at Barnabas but the bullets had no effect. He fired again and then Barnabas sprang on him and a terrible struggle began between the two. Diana watched with terror distorting her loveliness as the mad Count had the advantage for a second and then Barnabas. She could not tell how it would end.

And then somehow the Count was rolled close against the still blazing torch and his clothing picked up the flames. He screamed his terror as the yellow tongues began to envelop him. Barnabas released him and stood back. By this time the Count was a human torch. Diana pressed her hands over her eyes as he ran towards the mouth of the cave. She heard his last spine-tingling wail as he jumped to certain death.

Then Barnabas came to her and held her in his arms. "It's over," he said.

"I never dreamed it could be him," she sobbed brokenly, allowing her fears to show fully at last.

"I suspected it after I talked with Padrel. I knew there was someone behind him, urging him on in his evil. Padrel is a cheat but not diabolical enough to plan all that has been going on here. It had to be the hand of a master."

"And it was," she sighed. "Now how do we get safely out of this place?"

"We'll have no trouble," Barnabas promised her. "With the Count out of the way it will be no problem to handle Maria and her father."

She looked up at him solemnly. "The Count talked a good deal before he brought me down here," she said. "He made it plain Padrel is a faker. He has no cure for you, Barnabas."

"I realize that a little late," Barnabas said in a bitter tone. "It was his sole plan to have Maria marry me. Then they could control me and my fortune."

"What now?"

He shrugged. "What has it always been? I'll go on wandering." Her eyes met his. "But not alone."

The melancholy, handsome face showed tenderness. "How brave you are," he said. "How wonderful that I should find a lovely girl willing to share my isolation."

"We must leave tonight," she begged him.

"I will require another night to settle things here," he told her. "Then I will go."

"But if the villagers should find you in the meanwhile?"

"They won't," he smiled. "I have my hiding place in the cemetery and Peters to guard me. Let us go back upstairs."

They made their way up the stone steps and Barnabas led her through a corridor she'd not been in before. It took them to the front of the house. Barnabas motioned her to silence as they crept up on the scientist and his attractive daughter, who were standing talking in low tones in his study.

Then Barnabas thrust himself in the doorway and revealed himself to the startled two. "The Count is dead," he told them sternly.

"Your little game is over. You have until tomorrow noon to leave Collinsport."

Their white faces and shocked silence proved their guilt. Barnabas did not wait for a reply but quickly guided her to the front door and outside. They walked back to Collinwood, losing no time on the way. A safe distance from the house he halted and said goodnight to her.

After he'd kissed her, he said, "Go to Widows' Hill at dusk tomorrow night. I will be there."

And that was how they parted. She later recalled the moment of tenderness and love and wondered why she hadn't realized then what it meant. But so much had happened that night that her perception had been numbed.

The next day she heard from Jim Collins that Dr. Padrel and his daughter had hired a rig to drive them to the railway station at Ellsworth. They were going to take the train to Boston. Jim also reported about the finding of a body burned beyond recognition on the beach near the white house. This had started a lot of wild rumors again. But Barnabas need not stay at Collinwood any longer.

When dusk came at last she went to Widows' Hill and waited. And just as darkness became complete she heard someone coming along the cliff path towards her. Her heart gave a great bound of happiness as she went to meet Barnabas.

But it was not Barnabas who had come there. It was Dr. Stuben. The young doctor studied her with sad eyes. "I promised I would meet you here," he told her.

"Where is Barnabas?"

"He's gone. He left last night."

She was hurt and bewildered. "Without telling me? Surely he left a message. Did he say where we can meet?"

"There's to be no meeting," the young doctor said gently. "Barnabas asked me to tell you that. He loves you too much to want you to share his fate."

Tears brimmed in her eyes. "He didn't love me!"

"Don't ever say or think that," Robert Stuben reproved her. "Believe me, wherever Barnabas is now, and wherever his unhappy fate may lead him, you will always be in his heart."

The knocking on the door came to her more clearly. Stirring in bed, Maggie opened her eyes and saw that it was morning. Raising herself on an elbow, she glanced in the direction of the door.

"Yes?" she called out.

"It's Carolyn. You've overslept."

"Did I?" She wasn't fully awake yet. She glanced down at the coverlet and saw one of the ancient diaries still open there. "I read far later than I should have. Wait. I'll let you in." She got up and went over and unlatched the door.

Carolyn, already dressed, eyed the sleepy Maggie in her pajamas, and laughed. "It's not often I'm the one up first."

Maggie smiled. "I have a good alibi. I couldn't tear myself away from the diaries of that Diana Hastings." She went over to the bed and picked up the open one and, closing it, placed it on the side table with the others.

Carolyn eyed the books. "Were they interesting?"

"Very," she said with a nod. "I had some kind of a nightmare as well. Somehow it's all mixed up with what I read in the diaries."

The other girl sat on a chair arm. "What did you dream?"

Maggie shook her head. "I honestly can't remember now. It was as if a voice, the voice of Diana Hastings was telling me a long story. A story that wasn't included in the diaries I read."

"A new ghost voice at Collinwood! That's really something!" Carolyn mocked her.

She laughed. "It's what I get for reading so late."

"Who was this Diana Hastings?"

Maggie picked up one of the diaries and flicked through its pages. "She was an English girl who came here as a guest of Stephen Collins about eighty years ago. She stayed a short while and then returned to London. Later a young doctor from here named Robert Stuben joined her in England and they were married. She came back here after the First World War and left these diaries. She was an elderly woman then. I gather that she was only here for a brief visit after the death of her husband."

Carolyn smiled knowingly. "I'll bet there was a lot more to it than that. Diaries never tell all."

Maggie gave her an odd look. "No," she said quietly. "They don't."

COMING SOON FROM
HERMES PRESS

...and over a dozen more thrilling *Dark Shadows* editions!

DARK SHADOWS

Published by **Hermes** Press

COMING SOON

Dark Shadows: The Complete Series: Volume 1
SECOND EDITION
From the Gold Key Comics 1968-1970
www.hermespress.com

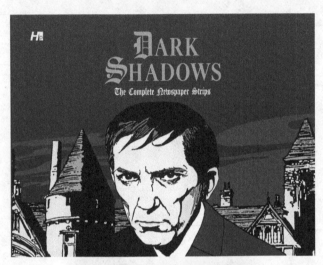
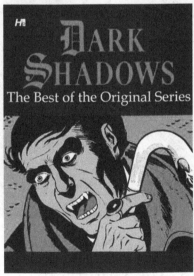